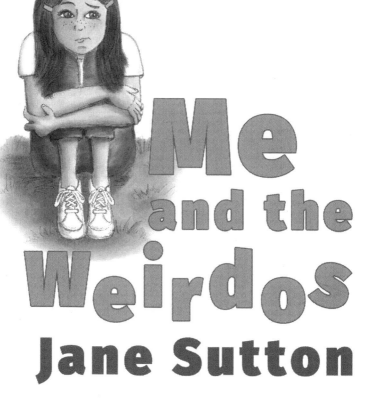

Me
and the
Weirdos

Jane Sutton

Illustrated by Doreen Buchinski

Original edition published in 1981 by Houghton Mifflin

ISBN: 978-1723370731

To Eva Perkins and Ashley Berrett,
whose wonderful musical *Me and the Krinkles*,
inspired me to get this book back in print

Chesterville, USA
1981

1

"Mom, Do You Think Our Family is Weird?"

When I was little, I thought everyone's family was like mine.

One day last spring, Roger Snooterman, the newspaper delivery kid in our neighborhood, came to drop off a bill. He rang our doorbell. It played the first seven notes of "Somewhere Over the Rainbow."

Just as I answered the door, my mother spun by doing cartwheels.

"*What* is your mother doing, Cindy?" Roger asked.

"She always does cartwheels," I said. "They're her favorite exercise."

"Your family is really weird," said Roger in a tone as snooty as his last name.

"They are not," I said.

"They are too! Your mother is the only grown-up who

wears red sneakers every day—in summer and winter. Even when it rains, you can see the red sneakers under her see-through boots."

"So what?" I said.

"So what?" answered Roger. "Aren't you embarrassed by the things your family does? Your father is the only person in Chesterville who rides a bike with an umbrella on it. And his bike horn plays the first four notes of *Frère Jacques*. Tell me *that's* not weird!"

"The umbrella keeps the rain and sun off his bald head," I said. "And the horn lets people know he's coming."

"People hear him coming anyway because he's always singing opera."

"He enjoys singing opera. Especially on his bicycle."

Roger rolled his eyes. "And let's not forget your sister," he said with a sneer. "Who else rides to school on roller skates, twirling a baton?"

"I don't know," I said, "I never thought about it before."

"Well, I have," said Roger. "I know all kinds of families because I deliver papers all over town. And believe me, yours is the weirdest."

With that last "compliment," Roger rode off on his bicycle. "Maybe there will be a weird family contest!" he called back. "Your family might win a free trip or something."

Roger Snooterman thought he was so smart just because he was a couple of years older than I was and was chosen the *Chesterville News* Delivery Kid of the Year two years in a row. I decided not to pay attention to what he said. I didn't like the way he went around sneering at everything. Besides, I loved my family, even my annoying sister.

On the other hand, Roger did know a lot of families. Could he be right about mine?

I thought about my family's names. Our last name *was* pretty weird—it was Krinkle. My father's first name was usually a last name—Smith.

I supposed my sister's and my middle names were unusual. Sarah's was Butterfly, and mine was Toucan, so we were Sarah Butterfly Krinkle and Cindy Toucan Krinkle.

My mother's first name was Squirrel. Before she got married, it was Crystal. But she didn't like the way Crystal Krinkle sounded, so she changed her name to Squirrel Krinkle.

I decided to ask Squirrel Krinkle herself about Roger Snooterman's opinion. She had finished doing cartwheels and was polishing the drinking fountain in our living room. I took a good look. Her frizzy gray hair stuck straight out, as usual. And of course, she was wearing red sneakers.

"Mom, do you think our family is weird?" I asked.

"Of course not," she said. "We're a wonderful family!" She went on to clean the gumball machine next to the drinking fountain. I had to admit that our furnishings were pretty unusual.

I went outside to talk to my father, who was working in the backyard.

It was true that my father didn't look like your everyday person. The top of his head was completely bald, but he had long black hair that started about an inch above his ears and hung down in a scraggly mess almost to his shoulders.

At the moment, he was planting dandelion seeds.

I looked around the yard, through Roger Snooterman's eyes. Our backyard had all kinds of weeds my father had planted. It also had about 50 million (well, maybe 12) bird-feeders he had made out of coconuts and old soda cans. And in the front yard, he and my mother had trimmed our bushes into the shape of two penguins and three rocket ships.

While my father continued burying dandelion seeds in the dirt, I told him that my best friend Patti's father *killed* the dandelions in his yard with chemicals. "Isn't it kind of weird to grow dandelions on purpose?" I asked.

"Not at all, Cindy Toucan," he said. "Dandelions are quite beautiful. Especially compared to dull, ordinary grass, which is always the same old green, except when it turns brown. And no one likes brown grass."

My father's weeds *were* pretty, I thought. A lot of them had colorful flowers. But I knew Roger Snooterman would say it was totally weird to go out of your way to grow plants

4

that most people tried to get rid of.

It was time to ask my sister what she thought about our family. Sarah, by the way, had big curly hair that looked like a red bird's nest. She was only 13, but she was almost as tall as our father.

I walked up to her door, which was decorated with labels from cans. Some big sisters collected stamps or coins or autographs. Patti's big sister used to collect posters of famous singers. But *my* big sister collected can labels. She especially liked mixed vegetables and creamed corn labels.

Since our mother hardly ever served canned food, Sarah had to go around asking people for empty cans so she could peel off the labels. Then she papered the walls of her room and her door with them.

I knocked on her door, imagining what Roger Snooterman would say about the labels on it.

"Who desires entrance and what is your purpose?" Sarah shouted—her usual greeting.

"It's Cindy," I called. "I want to ask you something. Do you think our family is weird?"

There was no answer.

"Sarah!" I shouted. "Did you hear me?"

"Don't disturb me," she finally answered. "I'm counting my baked beans labels."

Maybe Roger Snooterman is right, I thought.

There were lots of odd things about my family he didn't

even know about.

My father, for example, picked you up and twirled you around in a circle three times when he was glad to see you.

My mother gargled with orange juice three times a day. She said it kept her healthy.

Our family even had a strange pet. We didn't have a cat or a dog or a parakeet. No, we had a sea urchin, named Gomer. He was a little gray, round blob with spines all over him, and his mouth was in the middle of his bottom.

When Sarah found Gomer at the beach on a school field trip, she insisted on keeping him for a pet. She promised our parents she would change his water and add salt to it every day and feed him seaweed and chopped meat, and she did.

Gomer usually sat around in a bowl all day. When Sarah took him out of his bowl to play with him (I certainly didn't), she had to be very careful because his spines were sharp. Sea urchins usually don't have much personality, and Gomer was no exception.

Roger was right. The Krinkles were a weird family.

I started to worry that I was weird, too. But I didn't think I was. I thought of myself as a normal nine-and-a half-year-old. I worked hard at school. I liked to draw pictures and play the piano. I dressed neatly, and I had long brown hair that I usually wore with two barrettes. I had brown eyes and some freckles on my nose. I didn't think you could guess from looking at me that I lived with a bunch of weirdos.

Now I wondered how many people besides Roger Snooterman disliked my family. I wondered if I would lose my friends, even Patti, and my second best friend, Grant.

I decided I'd better do something fast. My mother, my father, and Sarah, didn't even know they were weird, so it would be a challenge to unweird them. But I had to!

Chomping on gum from the living room gumball machine, I wandered around the house thinking. After a while I came up with a plan—I would stop talking. When my family asked me why, I would answer, "Because you're all weird. And if you don't quit being weird, I'll *never* talk to you again."

I would start this unweirding plan the next morning.

For breakfast my mother cooked pancakes. Her pancakes were always delicious. And they came out in different shapes because she poured the batter into cookie cutters on the hot frying pan. We usually topped them with fresh fruit, except for Sarah, who ate them with tomato sauce and cheese. I know—weird!

Anyway, the fabulous smell of those pancakes just *got* to me, I guess. When my mother asked if I wanted fresh strawberries with them, I said, "Mmm, yes, please," before I remembered I was supposed to stay silent.

It was the end of my not talking plan. But the

duck-shaped pancakes with butter and fresh strawberries made having a weird family a little easier to swallow.

There must be another way to get them to stop being weird, I thought as I reached for a second helping.

2

The Impossible
Homework Assignment

Over the next few days, I tried to think of new unweirding ideas for my family. I wasn't getting anywhere.

Then my teacher, Mrs. Reed, gave us a difficult homework assignment. The assignment wasn't so hard for the rest of the class. But for me, it was just about impossible.

We were supposed to watch a TV program and write a review of it the next day during class. Mrs. Reed told us to write down the names of the actors and actresses and the roles they played, and the names of the director and writers. We had to take notes about what happened on the show and what the scenery and the music were like.

When we wrote the review, we would use our notes to describe the show and say if we liked it and why or why not.

Everybody in my class was excited to get to watch TV for a homework assignment.

9

"I'm gonna watch 'Journey to Planet Zetto,'" my friend Grant said with a grin.

"I think I'll watch 'The Bob and Bobby Show,'" a girl in my class said.

I was the only one *not* excited about the assignment. Remember I said it was just about impossible for me? That was because my family didn't own a TV! Some kids in my class had two. Patti's family had three TVs—a little one, a medium-sized one, and a giant one. We didn't even have one.

Why, you ask? Well, my parents believed it was bad to sit and stare at TV. They said it was better to be doing things than to watch people on TV doing things. I used to try to talk them into getting a TV, but I gave up. At least we had a record player and a radio. And I could watch TV when I visited Patti.

I went to Patti's house lots of days after school. She and I did just about everything together, except she belonged to the Young Raccoons and I belonged to the Young Blue Jays. Patti was really kind and funny. She was little and cute, with short blonde hair and bangs. Her family was nice, and they were not weird at all. So far, she liked to hang around with my family. I hoped that lasted.

When I got home, I had to wait to talk with my mother. She was in the basement giving fencing lessons, which she did three afternoons a week.

"What an interesting assignment!" she exclaimed, enthusiastic as usual.

"But I can't do it," I said.

"Why not?"

"Because we don't have a TV."

"We don't? Oh, I guess you're right."

My mother was on the absent-minded side. She said she was too busy doing things in the present to think about the past. But I reminded her that it was right now, in the present, that we didn't have a TV.

"Maybe you could watch TV at Patti's or Grant's house tonight," she suggested.

"I can't. Mrs. Reed wants us to watch by ourselves," I explained. "That way we'll watch lots of different shows. And we won't share our ideas before we write our reviews."

"Yes, forming your own views is important," said my mother. She poured a glass of orange juice. Throwing her head back, she made noises like a chicken with a bad headache.

When she finished gargling, I said, "What am I going to do about watching TV?"

"TV?" she said. "Oh, yes. Well ... since it's for a school assignment, we'll just have to rent one!"

Right away she called Rent-a-Thing in downtown

Chesterville and arranged to rent a TV for one night. My father would pick it up on his way home from work and strap it to his bicycle.

My father rode his bike to work every day, even when it snowed. He worked at the airport, about ten miles from our house. His job was to clean airplanes between flights. He liked his job because he worked alone most of the time, and he could sing opera as loud as he wanted. (He sang off-key, but he didn't seem to realize this.)

You know those air-sickness bags they give out on airplanes? My father brought the extras home, for me and Sarah to carry our lunches in. Sarah actually took her lunch to school in those bags. I did not.

———

At seven o'clock, it was time for "Comedy Corner," the TV special I had decided to watch. I got a notebook and sharpened a pencil, turned on the TV and sat down on a mattress. Oh, I forgot to mention this before—instead of sofas and chairs, our living room had mattresses, the furniture my parents decided was the most comfortable.

I waited for the TV to come on, but nothing happened.

"Daddy!" I called. "Nothing's happening."

"I think you have to let TVs warm up," he said. He was in the dining room singing opera as he watered flower pots of crabgrass he had transplanted from the yard.

I waited a while longer. Still nothing.

"Daddy! It's still not on. I'll miss the beginning of the show!"

He bounded into the living room and turned the On/Off button off and then on again. Nothing happened. He turned the channel selector to every channel, from 1 to 13. Nothing happened. He adjusted the antenna. The screen stayed blank.

"I'll miss the show, and I won't be able to do the assignment," I wailed.

My father dashed to the closet for his safari hat, one of those tan hats that explorers wear in the jungle. He claimed it helped him think because it kept thoughts from flying away. To me, he looked better than usual when he wore the hat. It hid the top of his bald head, which looked so strange with his long black hair.

Now my mother and Sarah plopped down on mattresses. When I told them the TV wouldn't go on, my mother called Rent-a-Thing for advice. Wearing his safari hat my father paced around the living room, glancing at the TV every once in a while.

Just as my mother came back, my father threw his hat up in the air and shouted, "I've got it!" He raced over to the TV and plugged it into the wall outlet. It turned on right away.

"Yay!" we all shouted.

"What did Rent-a-Thing say, Mom?" asked Sara.

"The manager asked if we plugged in the TV," said my

mother. "I said, 'Of course we did.'"

We all laughed. I felt a lot better now that I could watch most of the 90-minute special.

"I'll be back," my mother said. "I need to call Rent-a-Thing again."

"Why?" Sarah asked.

"Shh!" I said, "I'm trying to listen to the show."

"I want to tell the manager the TV wasn't plugged in after all," whispered my mother, who was very, very honest.

The first comedy skit was about a bagel shop that only served bagel holes. Customers were ordering onion bagel holes and poppy seed bagel holes and plain bagel holes. I wrote down some of the jokes in my notebook and which characters and lines I thought were the funniest.

My father said, "You know, a shop that serves just bagel holes is an interesting idea."

"It's supposed to be funny, Daddy," I said.

"How come you're talking?" Sarah asked me. "I thought you have to listen to the show."

I didn't bother to answer her.

My mother came back in exclaiming, "Some people! I told the Rent-a-Thing manager that the TV hadn't been plugged in after all, and I was sorry I'd said that it was plugged in when it really wasn't. And he said, 'Who cares?!' Some people just don't appreciate honesty."

When a commercial came on, my father turned the volume down low so we couldn't hear it. He said he didn't want Sarah and me to listen to commercials because they could talk you into anything, even things you'd be better off not having.

This inspired my father to get into one of his big word moods: "I am acquainted with a flight attendant who watched a cat food commercial," he said. "The commercial featured a charming, singing cat. She admired the cat so much, she immediately drove to the nearest pet food establishment and purchased an entire case of cat food. However ... she did not own a cat."

There was a commercial about a hamburger restaurant. Without any sound, it looked really funny. You could see people singing away, but no words were coming out of their mouths. Sarah made up a jingle—"Our hamburgers are so delicious ... and so nutritious ... we make them quick ... but you'll get sick!"

I couldn't help laughing.

Next came a commercial about an allergy medicine. A man was holding a bottle of the pills and speaking. My father talked along with the man's moving lips—"This allergy medicine is the greatest! It really ... *achoo* ... makes me ... *achoo* ... feel much ... *achoo* ... better."

When the show came back on, I turned the volume up. But Sarah said, "Let's leave the sound off. We can keep making up our own words."

"We can't! I have to listen to the show for homework."

"Just one skit," said Sarah. "It's so much fun!"

"OK. But just one."

The "just one" skit was about people camping in the wilderness. Sarah and my parents acted it out. My mother made noises like a wolf. Sarah talked along with the little girl. My father made up the words for one of the frightened campers. In his safari hat, he looked like a camper.

I tapped my foot, waiting to hear the actual show again.

When the next skit came on, I got up from the mattress to turn up the volume. "Oh, Cindy, don't be a party pooper," said Sarah.

"We agreed—just one skit!" I said. "I'm turning the sound on ..."

Sarah planted herself in front of the TV. "No!" she yelled.

"Yes!" I yelled louder. I tried to reach around her, but she pushed me away with her bony elbows.

"Girls, girls, a little less violence," said my father.

I tried to shove Sarah out of the way, but she stood there like a tall, skinny tree. We started swinging our arms at each other, and somehow, the TV got knocked over. *Crash*! As it hit the floor, I could hear something fall apart on the inside.

My father righted the TV. The picture was still on. That was good. But when he rotated the volume button, nothing happened. He turned it as far as it would go, but still we heard nothing. The sound was broken!

"Now look what you did!" I shouted.

"What *I* did!" my sister yelped. "You're the one ..."

"Stop fighting, girls," said my mother. "Now you see what problems TV watching leads to."

"Ha ha," said Sarah, aiming a smirk in my direction. '"We *have* to make up our own words to the skits now because we *can't* turn the sound on."

"Sarah Butterfly is right, Cindy Toucan," said my father. "We may as well enjoy ourselves acting out the skits."

"Can't you fix the sound?" I asked him in a small, trying-not-to-cry voice.

"If I take the TV apart to fix it, you'll miss the rest of the show," he said, putting an arm around my shoulders. "I will attempt to repair it later. You can *watch* the show for your homework assignment, even though you are not able to listen."

While my weird parents and sister returned to acting out skits, I took notes about the scenery and costumes. But how could I write my review without having heard the actors and actresses, or the sound effects, or the music? If Roger Snooterman were there, he would have said, "I told you your family is weirder than weird."

"Want to join in too, Cindy?" asked my mother. She grabbed me in a bear hug and kissed the top of my head.

"Yes, it is not every day that we Krinkles have a TV," my father pointed out to me.

"I don't feel like doing any acting," I said, scowling on my mattress seat.

The next skit took place in a hospital.

"I'm afraid we'll have to operate on your zookalooloo bone," announced Sarah when the doctor was on the screen.

"Goodness, no!" yelled my father when there was a close-up of the patient.

"Not the zookalooloo bone!" groaned my mother, the patient's wife.

My family acted out three more skits and five more commercials. They kept asking me to join them, but I refused.

The last skit was about astronauts going to the moon. Sarah and my mother did the voices of the astronauts. My father took on the voice of the launch control station: "Ten, nine, eight, seven, six ..."

"What can we bring you from the moon?" my mother, the astronaut, asked brightly before she blasted off.

"Some green cheese," requested my father. "Five, four, three, two, one, zero, blastoff!"

"Oh no, I forgot my can label collection!" Sarah the astronaut shrieked when the TV rocket ship was high in the sky. As the show ended, I copied down the names of the cast that scrolled down the screen. They went by so fast that I couldn't get them all written down, but I tried.

Now my mother and father and Sarah headed down to the basement because it was nine o'clock. This was another weird thing about my family—every night, from nine to nine-fifteen, they screamed together. My parents thought it was a good way to get rid of any bad feelings left over from the day. I used to do it, too. But after I found out they were weird, I started playing the grand piano in our kitchen instead, to drown out the screams.

When I remembered I would have to write the TV review the next day, I felt like screaming, too. But I didn't. I tried to concentrate on playing the piano, but I couldn't. I just sat on the piano bench and worried.

The next morning, as we entered the classroom, I whispered to Patti what happened. I knew I could trust her not to tell anyone about the weird things my family did.

"It's too bad you and Sarah had a fight," said Patti. "But acting out the skits sounds like fun. *My* parents just sat there and watched TV like they always do. It was dull city." City was one of Patti's favorite words. She said things were dull city, super city, horrible city, and lots of other cities.

"Things would be a lot easier if *my* family was dull city," I said. "How can I write the review when I didn't hear the show?"

Patti thought and then said in her little voice, "Write what you *did* hear. I bet what your family said was funnier than the show anyway."

"Mrs. Reed won't think so. She told us to listen and take

notes."

"You *tried* to listen. Wait ... I have an idea. You could write a review about what it's like to watch TV without the sound."

Then Mrs. Reed will know how weird my family is, I thought.

But I took Patti's advice because she was really smart in school, plus I couldn't think of a better idea. I wrote what I saw on TV and what I heard from my family. I described the scenery and the costumes. I listed the names of the cast and the director that went by at the end.

I didn't mention my shoving match with Sarah.

At the end of the review, I got a little carried away: "Watching TV without the sound is a new form of family entertainment," I wrote. "It helps develop your imagination."

Now I sound like a TV commercial, I thought as I read it over, but I hoped for the best.

Mrs. Reed read our reviews while we were in gym and handed them back at the end of the day. I took a deep breath before I looked at her comments: "Excellent job, Cindy. Well-written, with good details. You made me feel as if I were there!"

Phew. Way better than I expected.

But I didn't think Mrs. Reed really meant what she wrote. She probably said those nice things because she felt sorry for a kid in such a weird family.

3

How to Unweird a Family

I hated to admit that Roger Snooterman was right. But he was—my family was definitely embarrassing.

How could I stop them from being weird? My silence plan hadn't lasted through one pancakes-with-strawberries breakfast. But if I got them to try acting normal, even once, they might like it and decide to make acting normal a habit.

The next Saturday was an unusually warm day for May. In the front yard, my father was planting dandelions as he sang opera off-key. My mother hummed happily as she trimmed the rocket ship and penguin-shaped bushes. Sarah roller-skated up and down the driveway, twirling her baton.

I sat on the front steps trying to think of a normal activity for my family—a normal activity with normal people around. Maybe they stayed weird because they were around each other so much that they didn't see what regular families did.

Just then a convertible drove by. The kids in the back had pails, shovels, inflated rafts, and flippers.

The beach!

I couldn't even remember the last time we Krinkles had gone to the beach. In the summer I often went with Patti to her parents' swimming pool club. Everybody acted normal there.

The beach seemed like the perfect place to unweird my family. Surrounded by normal people, they'd be sure to catch on how to act normal, too!

I ran over to my parents, shouting, "Let's go to the beach!"

My father instantly got into one of his big-word moods: "You, Cindy, are a true inspiration. There is nothing quite so lovely as the beach—the magical environment where land meets water. And incidentally, my increasing perspiration as I labor with these plants makes the idea additionally appealing."

"I haven't been to the beach in years," said my mother, throwing down her pruning shears. "Let's go!"

Sarah was excited about the beach, too, which was surprising, since it had been my idea.

We changed into beach clothes and piled into our van, which my family had painted with flowers and robots as soon as they bought it.

We were about to leave when my mother said, "Wait a

minute!" She jumped out and circled the van three times. As she ran, she flapped her elbows like a bird and crowed. Luckily, we were still in our driveway. I didn't think anyone saw her. Or heard her.

Back in the van, she caught her breath and said, "Now we will have good weather at the beach. That was a sun dance one of my fencing students taught me."

On the road towards the beach, a teenaged hitchhiker was holding a cardboard sign that said "Beach."

My father pulled the van over to pick her up. She climbed in saying, "Thank you very much!" Then she looked at the driver and got quiet. She started shaking.

I didn't blame her for feeling scared. My father was wearing his safari hat to keep the sun off the bald top of his head. His arms were covered with hand-painted watercolor tattoos—bears and giraffes along his left arm, and along his right arm, "Have you hugged an airplane cleaner today?"

As for my mother, she had on a pink ballerina tutu and her red sneakers. Her gray frizzy hair stuck out more than ever.

The hitchhiker took a quick glance behind her at Sara, who was wearing a big purple hat over her bright red hair *and* her karate suit.

I had a normal one-piece bathing suit on. But I guess one normal person can't cancel out three weirdos. The hitch-hiker stared straight ahead, out the windshield. Her lips

24

were moving a little. Maybe she was praying.

As he drove, my father gave the hitchhiker a lecture. He told her she should never hitchhike again. "First of all, hitchhiking is against the law," he said. "Plus, you never know what kind of strange people will pick you up."

"I know what you mean," muttered the hitchhiker.

When we pulled into the beach parking lot, she grabbed her beach bag and her cardboard sign and opened the door.

"Wait just a minute," said my father.

The hitchhiker kept her trembling hand on the door handle as she turned towards him.

"Please do not ever hitchhike again," he said in a gentle voice.

"I won't," the hitchhiker said. "I promise."

"Here's some money to use for a bus ride home," he said. "There's a bus stop next to the snack bar."

The hitchhiker stared at him as she took the money. Stuffing it into her shorts pocket, she said, "Thanks." She jumped out of the van and sprinted for the beach.

My family may have cured her of ever even *thinking* of hitchhiking again.

We found a good spot on the beach, right near the water. I was hoping my family would look around and get the idea of what you're supposed to do at the beach. People were wading, sunbathing, listening to music, playing cards, throwing frisbees ...

"Who wants to play catch?" I asked. "I brought a beach ball. We can throw it around, and maybe some other people will play with us!"

"Perhaps later," said my father. "I am eager to fly the new kite I made."

And he did. Of course, it wasn't a normal-looking kite, like a diamond or a bird or a butterfly. No, my father's kite looked like a hamburger. In fact, he had named it The Flying Hamburger.

My mother didn't want to play catch either. She was busy practicing cartwheels in the sand.

Sarah just wanted to read the dictionary she brought. I looked at her and shuddered. I knew she needed long pants and sleeves to protect her pale skin from the sun. A karate suit at the beach was already weird, but did she have to wear mittens and take them off each time she turned a page?

I could feel people staring at us. I wanted to bury my head in the sand like an ostrich. But I lay on the beach blanket and pretended to be enjoying the sun.

After a while, I heard a commotion. I looked up and saw my father struggling with The Flying Hamburger. It had fallen on a frisbee player, who was now tangled in the string. As soon as the frisbee player managed to get untangled, he and the three other players ran off to another part of the beach.

When my father put The Flying Hamburger away, I popped up from the blanket. Now was my chance to encourage my family to do something normal. The water was too cold for swimming. So I suggested, "How about going wading?"

"Yes, let's try out the Queen Miranda!" said my mother.

"Aye aye, Captain," replied my father with a salute.

I hadn't realized that my mother had packed her toy boat. It was bad enough that she played with the Queen Miranda at home in the bathtub. But now she was going to play with it on a public beach, where everyone could see her! I decided I didn't want to wade with my parents after all.

Sitting back down on the beach blanket, I watched them and cringed. Each time the toy boat got tossed around in the waves, they giggled and clapped their hands. They made lots of noise being enthusiastic. "Whee! Oops, it almost sank! Go, Queen Miranda!"

I pulled a book out of my beach bag. But I couldn't focus and kept starting over on the same sentence.

After a while, I gave up trying to read and gazed around. I counted 14 people sitting near us. Fourteen, plus four frisbee players, plus one hitchhiker—that made 19 more people who now knew, without a doubt, that the Krinkles were weird. This beach outing was not working out as I had hoped.

I looked over at the family next to us. Under a yellow and green beach umbrella a grandmother was playing with a baby. A mother and grandfather were sitting in beach chairs, reading magazines. They all wore normal bathing suits. No karate suits, no ballerina tutus. Why couldn't my family be normal, like them?

The people on the other side of us were grilling hot dogs and hamburgers. They had the right idea—*eat* hamburgers, don't fly one! I wished my family were as normal as that group. They even had a regular-looking dog. I was sure they didn't have some dumb sea urchin at home.

I tried asking Sarah if she wanted to help me dig a big hole and bury each other in it. It seemed like a very normal thing to do at the beach.

She wouldn't even look up from her dictionary. "Don't bother me," she said. "I want to finish the B's today."

My parents were still playing gleefully with the Queen Miranda. At least my father's watercolor tattoos had washed off in the water.

"Hey, Cindy, come play with the boat!" my mother, the beach ballerina, called.

Immediately, I lay down and pretended to be asleep. If I didn't answer, no one would know the woman in a tutu was talking to me.

I guess my parents got tired of the toy boat after a while. They returned to the blanket, and I heard my father say, "I will embark on a walk. A leisurely ramble along the beach is both relaxing and exhilarating."

My mother stretched out on the blanket, next to me. Noticing that I was "asleep," she whispered to Sarah, "My sun dance must have worked. The weather is just beautiful—Cindy already has some cute new freckles on her nose."

Sarah didn't answer. She was studying the "B" words.

My mother snuggled next to me. She seemed to fall asleep, and I did, too. I had a dream that Roger Snooterman was counting my freckles and laughing his mean laugh.

———————

When I woke up, the family near us had left, and my mother was packing up the Queen Miranda and The Flying Hamburger. "It must be getting late," she said. "I'm hungry." My mother never wore a watch. She went on stomach time.

"Where's Daddy?" I asked.

"He hasn't gotten back from his walk yet," said my mother.

Sarah closed the dictionary and called, "Daddy-O! Daddy-cakes!"

"Can't you just call him Daddy?" I hissed. My face felt red. Not just from sunburn.

"Don't be ridiculous, Cindy," said Sarah. "If I yell 'Daddy,' every father on the beach will turn around."

As far as I could tell, every father on the beach *was*

turning around And so was every mother, sister, brother, aunt, and uncle—all gaping at the shouting redheaded girl in a purple hat, karate suit and mittens.

"Daddy-O! Daddy-cakes!" bellowed Sarah.

Then, unfortunately, we heard an even louder voice— the lifeguard talking over his bullhorn. "Attention, please! I have a lost man here. He's about 45 years old ... "

Next to the lifeguard on the tall white chair stood my anxious-looking father.

"He's wearing a safari hat ..." the lifeguard continued.

"Smith!" cried my mother.

"And he answers to the name, Smith Krinkle!" boomed the lifeguard.

My mother took off toward the lifeguard. When my father spotted the familiar figure in the pink tutu, he waved wildly and clambered down from the tall chair. He and my mother hugged. He picked her up and twirled her around three times because he was so glad to see her.

Everybody on the beach cheered and roared with laughter.

With their arms around each other, my parents strolled over to Sarah and me.

"I knew our blanket was next to a yellow and green umbrella, but I couldn't find it," my father said apologetically. "I guess the family with that umbrella went home."

The people who hadn't gone home yet were still laughing as they looked at us.

I am mortified, I thought.

I wasn't sure if *mortified* was the right word for the way I felt. While Sarah was busy clapping her mittened hands and exclaiming, "I'm so happy to see you, Daddy-cakes!"— I checked in her dictionary: "*Mortify*—to hurt someone's pride or self-respect."

I was mortified all right.

We packed up to leave. I was grateful for one thing—we hadn't run into anyone we knew.

I needed a different plan.

4

Foreign Behavior

I still believed my family could give up their weird ways if they had a chance to be normal. One afternoon on the beach was too short a time, I decided. So I stayed on the lookout for longer unweirding opportunities.

One day at school, Mrs. Reed handed out a notice asking families to have an international student stay with them. Chesterville had a chance for a student from France to visit us for two weeks if a host family could be found.

I wanted my family to volunteer. Hosting an international student seemed like a nice, normal thing to do. Even the Krinkles would know to be on their best behavior around a visitor from another country, I figured.

For the plan to work, they would need to be unweird for two weeks. If things worked out, they could try being normal for three weeks, and then maybe forever! When I brought home the notice, my father got into a big-word mood. "Excellent! Excellent!" he said. "The interconnecting of international cultures is a highly worthy goal, and I fully support this proposal."

My mother thought it would be lovely to get to know someone from another country.

Sarah was less than enthusiastic, partly because she hadn't thought of it first. "Where is this French student going to sleep?" she asked with a Roger Snooterman-like sneer.

"Well," said my mother, "your room is bigger than Cindy's, and we can move one of the living room mattresses into it."

"I don't like people near my can label collection," said Sarah. "I won't be able to watch this stranger every minute. The last time someone was in my room without me, six creamed corn labels were missing afterwards."

"Sarah Butterfly, my dear," said my father, "it is wonderful that you have developed your own highly original hobby. And it is commendable that you train your eyes to study the variations among can labels. But I think you may exaggerate the interest that other people have in your collection."

"In other words," I said, "no one is going to steal your labels because no one cares about your stupid collection."

"Cindy, please remember to be kind," said my mother.

"I'm sorry I used the word 'stupid,'" I said. "You don't

34

have to worry about anyone stealing your can labels."

"I am totally against our hosting a student," declared Sarah.

That's how I knew I was totally for it. Sarah and I disagreed about almost everything. So if she was against it, I knew it must be OK.

The French student coming to our house was named Marguerite. We all drove to the airport in the van to pick her up. On the way, I asked my family, "You'll all be on your best behavior, right?"

"We'll show Marguerite a wonderful time," said my mother. "Because we're a wonderful family!"

The first thing my father did when we got to the airport was put on a French beret. It pressed down on his head, making his black, stringy hair look even longer than usual.

"Daddy! Why are you wearing that?" I asked.

"I want to make Marguerite feel at home," he said grinning.

Marguerite's flight was right on time. When we met her after Customs, I thought she looked sweet but shy. Her eyes were a pretty gray-blue.

"Allo," she said softly. I liked her French accent.

I shook Marguerite's hand and said hello.

My mother gave her a bear hug that could knock you out for a month. My father picked her up and twirled her around in a circle three times.

I was afraid Marguerite would want to get right back on the plane. But she acted as if everything was fine. She even smiled a little.

Sarah asked her, "How come they call French fries 'french fries'?"

"Excuse me," Marguerite answered. "I do not understand what you mean."

Sarah was not about to leave this topic—"French fries! You *must* know about them. You're French, and they're French."

"I think French fries is an American term, Sarah," said my mother. "I also think we should go home now. Marguerite must be very tired and hungry."

I was pleased that my mother was acting so sensibly. As for Sarah, I gave her a dirty look. But it was lost on her. She was busy bothering my father about why they never put French fries in cans.

Back at the house, we ate dinner right away. My mother had cooked a vegetable stew. As usual, we all ate out of one pot, which sat in the middle of the table. We used wooden spoons that had extra-long handles. My parents thought it made us a closer family to eat dinner out of one pot.

Marguerite didn't say anything about our weird eating arrangement. "Zeese stew eese very much deeleecious," she said. "What are some zings zat are een it?"

"I don't really remember," said my mother. "Let me look ... I see potatoes ... onions ... peppers, tomatoes, turnips, celery, zucchini ... There seems to be just about every vegetable you could think of in this pot, except broccoli."

"You do not eat broccoli in zeese countree?" Marguerite asked as she took another spoonful of stew.

"Broccoli has so much personality, it seems mean to eat it," said my mother.

After dinner, my parents suggested one of their favorite activities—painting a mural on the living room wall. Most parents hung paintings in frames on their walls. Or photos or quilts. But *my* family painted right on the wall.

We used to have a mural of a jungle with monkeys, parrots, and crazy-looking trees. Our latest was a farm—with cows, pigs, chickens, a barn, and rows of vegetables. To get ready for Marguerite's visit, my father had covered over the farm with white paint.

Before I found out my family was weird, I had enjoyed painting on the wall. But lately I didn't want any part of it.

Now my father draped plastic sheets on everything in the living room—the mattresses, the water fountain, and the gumball machine.

"You are going to paint on zee wall?" asked Marguerite.

"*Mais oui!*" said my father. "That means, 'But yes!' in French, he told the rest of us. "What would you like to paint, Marguerite?"

"Maybe she doesn't feel like painting on a wall," I said. "Maybe she would like to see a movie. There's a rated PG movie playing at the Chesterville Cinema."

"I would love to paint with you," said Marguerite. "I do not know *what* to paint."

My father knew what *he* wanted to paint. We all watched as he started using black paint to make something very tall. It was skinny on the top and fatter on the bottom.

"The *Tour Eiffel*!" exclaimed Marguerite, smiling.

"*Mais oui*!" said my father. "Let's all paint scenes of France."

My mother painted a bakery with long French breads. Sarah painted a grocery store with cans in the window (of course) that said "French onion soup" and "French style green beans." Marguerite painted her house back home. It had black balconies and big windows.

Since everybody was acting weird anyway, I decided I might as well grab a paint brush. Along the top of the wall I painted a sign that said "Welcome, Marguerite!"

"Oh, zank you, Cindee," said Marguerite, her gray-blue eyes sparkling.

Marguerite seemed happy enough, but I kept thinking how odd my family must have seemed to her. She was very polite though. She acted as if she enjoyed painting on the wall with us.

At nine o'clock it was time for the nightly screaming

session. By then I figured Marguerite must have figured out that she had ended up with a really loony host family. But she said screaming out bad feelings sounded like a good idea, and she went down to the basement to join in. I played piano in the kitchen.

Fifteen minutes later, they marched up from the basement with big smiles. When my mother asked Marguerite if she wanted to try the shower in our backyard, she said, "Yes!"

Marguerite was agreeing to *every* weirdo suggestion. I thought she was super brave, especially since she must have been tired from traveling all the way from France.

She declared that the outdoor shower, which my father had made out of an old ice cream truck, was "*magnifique.*" Afterwards, she settled onto the living room mattress now on the floor of Sarah's room. Sarah made her promise not to touch any of her can labels.

I wondered if you could get fired from being a host family.

————

The rest of Marguerite's stay went by really fast. Every day after school we took her sightseeing. We went to parks and museums. At night we went to the movies and to our favorite restaurants in Chesterville.

I was encouraged that my family acted normal a lot of the time. And when they did weird things, Marguerite would say, "How eenteresting!"

We taught her how to play the pretend orchestra game, one of my family's favorite things to do. We put on music and pretended to play different instruments. Marguerite seemed to love it, especially when she took her turn playing the bass drum.

She also came with me to one of my Young Blue Jays meetings. My Young Blue Jays group met every Friday afternoon. We did all kinds of normal activities. We did crafts, put on plays, took hikes, and lots of other unweird stuff. Marguerite talked to the group about life in France. She liked the girls, and they liked her.

While Marguerite stayed with us, school was fun. On the playground, everybody wanted to hang out with both of us. At lunch, kids asked her about France, and they asked me what it was like to host an international student. Mrs. Reed made a big deal about how generous my family was to volunteer for the program.

At home we had more visitors than usual while Marguerite was around. Grant visited us after school twice. Patti came along sightseeing sometimes and out to a restaurant one night.

Even Roger Snooterman stopped at the door to chat one day when he delivered the newspaper. Luckily, my parents were reading quietly in the living room (almost like normal parents, except they were sitting on mattresses).

Of course, Roger couldn't leave without reminding me what he thought of my family. "I wonder how they let *your* family host an international student," he said.

I didn't answer. It was actually a good question. But what Roger didn't realize was that the Krinkles, thanks to my unweirding plan, were on the road to being normal!

———————

By the time Marguerite went home, I felt my family had done a really good job as hosts. Marguerite had had a great time with us. She cried when she left. We all did.

A couple of weeks later, though, I cried for a different reason. School was over for the summer, and I had spent the day at Patti's parents' swimming pool club. When I got home, Sarah was all excited. She was next to the living room gumball machine twirling her baton so fast I could barely see it. "We're in the paper!" she shouted.

As her baton clattered to the floor, she turned to page three of the *Chesterville News* and showed me this:

FRENCH STUDENT WRITES ABOUT CHESTERVILLE TRIP

Our French visitor, Marguerite Lyonnet, has graciously sent the *Chesterville News* an article she wrote for her hometown paper in France. Last month, Marguerite was a guest of the Krinkle family for two weeks. Here is the article, translated by

Ms. Alberta Possum of the Chesterville High School French Department:

I had a wonderful time in the United States. My host family was so sweet to me!

I learned many interesting things about Americans. Did you know that they all eat from one pot at dinner? Also, they do not eat broccoli because it seems like a human. When Americans make a peanut butter sandwich, they put the peanut butter on the outside and the bread on the inside. That is so you can taste the peanut butter more.

Every night the American family gets together and screams. It makes you feel better. I tried it, too.

The American women are very strong. They hug you hard. For exercise they do cartwheels. To be healthy they gargle with orange juice.

The men ride to work on bikes with umbrellas on them. Also, the men wear berets, just like in France.

Americans take showers in their backyards. The children collect can labels and keep sea urchins for pets.

Sadly, I did not have a chance to spend time in the homes of any other American families besides my hosts. But if other Americans are like Smith, Squirrel, Sarah, and Cindy Krinkle in Chesterville, the United States is a very nice and a very different country.

One more thing: To wake them up in the morning, Americans have alarm clocks that say cock-a-doodle-doo.

"Isn't that a cool article?" asked Sarah. "She remembers everything about us!"

I didn't answer. I was too busy sobbing.

"Just because she talked about my can label collection, Cindy, and she hardly wrote a word about *you* is no reason to cry. You could start a collection, too. How about different kinds of tissue boxes?"

Hosting Marguerite did not unweird my family at all, I thought miserably. *And now that she praised their odd behavior, they'll never want to change.*

Even worse, the whole world would read how weird they were—at least everybody in Chesterville and everybody in France.

5

One Weirdo at a Time

I couldn't stop thinking about Marguerite's article in the *Chesterville News*. I felt horrible, awful ... mortified about it. The one good thing was that it came out during summer vacation, so I didn't have to face anyone at school.

For the whole next week I stayed around the house so I wouldn't run into anybody. When Roger Snooterman delivered the paper, I hid in the coat closet. If he saw me, I just knew he'd say my family had given French people a bad impression of the United States. He would say Chesterville wouldn't be allowed to host any more international students and it was all my family's fault.

I didn't feel like hanging out with my friends. Grant was away at summer camp anyway. I could have gone with Patti to her parents' swimming pool club, but I didn't want to. I didn't go to my next Young Blue Jays meeting either. I was afraid one of the girls would say, "I hear you have an alarm clock that says cock-a-doodle-doo," and the rest of the Young Blue Jays would burst out laughing.

One afternoon I was in the backyard throwing a tennis ball against the outdoor shower. It felt good to throw hard, and the ice cream truck sides made a loud noise that matched my wanting-to-scream mood.

"Cindy, you have a visitor!" called my mother, her frizzy gray head popping out the window.

It was Patti.

"Hi," I said, but I didn't look at her. I kept hurling the ball against the shower.

"What's wrong?" asked Patti. "I left a message with Sarah, and you didn't call me back. You look like angry city."

"Did you see the article in the *Chesterville News*?"

"Yeah," said Patti, giggling.

"Well, *that's* what's wrong. Everyone must be laughing at us. *You* just started laughing when I brought it up."

"Some of it *was* funny. But your family is great! They're nice, they're imaginative, they're interesting ... "

"*You* don't have to live with them," I said throwing the ball even harder. "*You* don't have to be seen with them! They're soooo weird!"

"They're the happiest people I know," said Patti, placing one of her little hands gently on my shoulder.

"That's because they're too weird even to know they're weird."

Patti took the tennis ball from my hand. I had been squeezing it as if I was desperate to get juice out of an orange. She tossed it back to me and said softly, "You have fun with your family, right? Just a little?"

"No. Not anymore anyway. I'm too worried about what other people think of them."

"Well, I may be short, but I *am* a person," said Patti smiling. "And I love your family, even if they are ... well ... different."

"How could you like people who make peanut-butter sandwiches with the peanut butter on the outside?" I grumbled, throwing the ball back to her.

"How could you not like them?"

We both laughed. I felt my scrunched up shoulders relax as I realized that my best friend still wanted to be around me and the weirdos.

Then Patti came up with an idea. "If you're really sick of your family," she said, "you can come live with *mine*. We have an extra bedroom now that my sister got married."

"Your parents wouldn't want me to live with them."

"Sure, they would. Every time you come over, my father says, 'That Cindy is a good kid.' Even my Aunt Luba likes you, and she hardly likes anyone."

"I'm not ready to give up on my family yet," I said. "My project for summer vacation is to come up with a new and improved unweirding plan. But thanks for the offer, Patti."

The plan I came up with was to work on my family one weirdo at a time. I decided it had been a mistake to take on the whole family at once. No wonder going to the beach and hosting an international student hadn't worked! In my new plan, I would give each person all my attention.

My mother would be first. Once she was normal, she could help me unweird my father. And when he was normal, both of them could help me work on Sarah ...

A few days later, my mother caught a cold. My mother is strange enough when she's healthy, but when she's sick—oh boy.

The morning she came down with a cold, she and I were alone in the house. My father had bicycled off to work, and Sarah had roller skated to an advanced baton-twirling class.

My plan was to teach my mother to be sick like everybody else.

"You need plenty of rest," I told her.

Since her nose was stuffed up, her answer sounded like: "I doe it, Ciddy. You're right."

She climbed into bed and said she would stay there until she felt better. She promised me that she wouldn't do any cartwheels. She even canceled her fencing classes for the rest of the day.

I thought I was making progress.

"When you have a cold, you need to drink a lot," I reminded her.

"You're right again," she said. She promised to gargle with orange juice every 15 minutes. I figured gargling was almost the same as drinking.

"How about taking medicine?" I suggested. "The last time I was at Patti's, I saw a TV commercial for Cold-Away Pills. They soothe colds in six different ways."

"Oh, I have better rebedies thad pills," she said.

I left her alone to rest. In my room, I wrote a post card to Grant at summer camp.

After a while, I checked on my patient. What I found was disappointing. She was already back to her weird ways. Yes, she was resting in bed, but she was wearing her special "sick hat"—made out of wads of cotton—that she claimed helped headaches. She was leafing through her album of restful photos—cows, cats and rhinoceroses lying down—to make herself feel peaceful.

To help her breathe better, she had brought some of the weed plants from the dining room and arranged them around her bed. Besides all these "rebedies," she was playing a recording of my father singing opera. There was a big smile on her face. With the thick cotton "sick hat" covering her ears, my father's singing must have sounded less dreadful.

"Why can't you be sick like other people, Mom?" I shouted above the so-called music. "They take pills! They sleep! They watch game shows on TV!"

"You'll see, Ciddy, I'll be better toborrow," she said. "By the way, please brig be by orange juice. "It's tibe for be to gargle again."

The next day, believe it or not, she was not just better, but *all* better. She hopped out of bed, tied up her red sneakers, gave five fencing lessons, and practiced cartwheels outside for an hour.

How could I get my mother to give up her weird sickness remedies if they worked?

––––––––––––––

Now that she was well, I decided to try something else. A baked goods and plant sale was coming up to raise money for the Chesterville PTA. Working at a PTA sale seemed like a very normal thing for a parent to do. So I asked my mother if she wanted to be part of it.

"Yes! Yes! Yes!" was her answer.

I offered to help her get ready for the sale, but she said she would rather surprise me with what she came up with. This sounded dangerous, but she politely and stubbornly refused to let me take a peek at her preparations.

The day before the sale, she baked for hours. You know the expression "bake up, or something up, a storm"? Well, she baked up a hurricane. And all night, she was down in the basement, potting plants to sell.

I was glad she was making such an effort for the PTA

sale. It seemed like an important start to my unweirding-my-first-weirdo plan.

At the sale, in Chesterville Town Hall, I walked around while she set up. The cakes and brownies and the flowers looked and smelled great.

Then the sale began. A big crowd gathered around my mother's table. She was beaming. I was not.

The items she had worked on in secret were not normal at all. They were the opposite of normal. She had baked giant cookies decorated like clocks and breads shaped like elephants. And her plants ... my stomach did a cartwheel when I saw them. She was selling dandelion plants.

While I was staring at my mother's table, someone jabbed me on the shoulder. It was Roger Snooterman. I was as glad to see him as I was when my doctor told me I had to get a booster shot.

"Hi Cindy," he said with his usual sneer. "I helped my mother set up her table. If I knew yours would be here, I would have made a special sign for *hers*—'Weirdo Table.'"

I didn't answer. I hoped he would go away.

But Roger had more to say. "Have you seen *my* mother's table? Oh, I guess you wouldn't be interested. She's selling roses, not weeds."

As Roger walked off with a mean laugh, I wanted to karate kick myself for not insisting on helping my mother get ready for the sale.

Now I stood at the edge of the crowd at her table, as unable to move as if *I* were a plant. I listened to the different comments: "What imaginative cookies and breads! What *strange* cookies and breads! What?—a dandelion for a house plant? I never realized how pretty dandelions are!"

At the end of the sale, the president of the PTA marched over to my mother. I thought she would tell her to stick to chocolate-chip cookies and daisy plants next time. I tried to look on the bright side: Maybe getting a lecture from the PTA president would actually help my unweirding plan. It would teach her a lesson!

Instead, the PTA president thanked my mother. She said my mother's baked goods and plants had made more money for the PTA than any other table.

"Next time, I'll bake my porcupine cookies, too," my mother said grinning.

"That would be terrific, Squirrel!" said the PTA president.

I was furious with the PTA. Here I was trying to get my mother to act normal, and the PTA president was thanking her for being weird.

———————

Even though my mother was still weird, I decided to go ahead and work on my father. If I could get *him* to be normal, he could help me work on my mother again.

The next Saturday I asked my father to go with me to

the library, which seemed like a perfect unweirding place. For one thing, since he would have to talk quietly, no one besides me would hear him if he said something weird. And a father and daughter going to the library together was such a normal activity. I could already hear myself saying after our successful day, "Isn't it fun to act like a regular person, Daddy?"

He said he would be pleased to go with me and even agreed to walk instead of riding his umbrella bicycle.

Sarah wanted to come, too, and take out a new book on sea urchins. I told her I would buy her two cans of creamed corn for her label collection if she stayed home. She said it was a deal.

The Chesterville Library had a new exhibit of antique toys. As my father and I looked at the exhibit, he was nice and quiet. He whispered to me about which toys he liked best. *So far, so good.*

Then my father noticed the metal toy trucks and cars. He started gently pushing one of the trucks to make it roll.

"Daddy! Stop it!" I hissed.

He stopped pushing. Unfortunately, he began opening its doors. "Experience how well-made the tiny door handles are," he said.

"You're not supposed to handle things in the exhibit," I said. "Look—the sign says 'Please don't touch.'"

"Oh, thank you for pointing that out, Cindy Toucan,"

he said. And he didn't handle anything else in the exhibit. I was encouraged that he was following the rules about not touching things and about being quiet. He just needed to be alone with someone normal, like me, to learn how to behave. With weirdos like my mother and Sarah around him all the time, no wonder he acted weird, too!

After we finished admiring the toy exhibit, we headed for the children's department. My Young Blue Jays group was planning a field trip to a fish hatchery, so we found a book with pictures of fish and looked through it together. My father kept his voice low. He seemed to enjoy acting like a normal person in a library!

I was about to congratulate him when a bunch of little kids toddled in for story hour. They sat down on a rug, around the children's librarian.

The librarian began to read them the story of Little Red Riding Hood. As she read each page, she held up the book to show them the pictures. Some of the little kids weren't listening. They were squirming around and poking each other.

My father frowned. "That librarian makes the story sound so dull," he whispered to me. "She reads with no expression."

"Look at this colorful fish, Daddy," I said pointing in the book. I wanted to get his mind off the story hour. I didn't like the look in his eyes.

"So Little Red Riding Hood filled the picnic basket with goodies to take to her grandmother," the librarian was saying. "Pay attention, Robbie and Steven!"

My father handed me the fish book and charged over to the story-hour group. "If you have no objection," he said to the librarian, "I'll help make the story a little more interesting."

"I don't know—" the librarian started to say.

"Don't let me interrupt you," my father interrupted her. "Go right on reading."

The librarian began reading again in her dull tone. And my father acted out the story. Whenever the librarian said "Little Red Riding Hood," he walked on his knees, smiling. When she said "the wolf," he moved around on all fours making a fierce face.

Robbie and Steven stopped squirming and poking each other. None of the other little kids fooled around anymore either. They were too busy listening to the story and watching the man with long black hair hanging down from his bald head.

He acted out all the parts—Little Red Riding Hood walking through the woods, the wolf hiding behind trees and pretending to be the grandmother in bed, and the woodsman running after the wolf with an axe.

At the end of the story, the kids cheered. "Can you come to story hour again, mister?" one of them asked.

"Yes! Come again!" the other kids shouted.

"Let's go home, Daddy," I said.

"I'm not ready to leave yet," he said, looking at the librarian, who was putting "Little Red Riding Hood" back on the shelf. "I want to ask when the next story hour will be."

Until that moment, I never knew how strong I was. I grabbed my father's hand and just about dragged him out of the library.

"I guess you really wanted to leave," boomed my father when we were safely outside. "That was very enjoyable. Did you notice how quiet I was? I whispered the whole time, and while I acted out Little Red Riding Hood, I didn't say one word!"

As we walked home, I hardly said a word either. I didn't feel like talking to the Story Hour interrupter. Besides, I was already trying to think of a way to unweird Sarah.

Maybe my parents were too old and set in their ways to be unweirded first. But Sarah was young. If I could get *her* to be normal, she and I could be a team and unweird our parents together.

Before we went home, my father and I bought the two cans of creamed corn I had promised Sarah for her label collection.

6

Blankets and Pizza on a Cold Summer Night

I waited for a chance to be alone with Sarah so I could get her started on normal activities. When she found out how much fun it was to do regular things, she might give up her can label collection, dictionary reading, and wearing karate suits everywhere. Maybe she would even trade Gomer for a dog.

One night in August, our parents decided to go out for one of their backwards dinners (desserts first, appetizers last). Sarah and I would be on our own!

"Where are you going out to eat?" Sarah asked our parents.

"First, we'll eat ice cream at Cone Town. Then we'll have a pear pie at Sally's Bakery," said my father.

"After that, we'll head to Burgers Unlimited for burgers," said my mother. "Then on to Salad Salad Salad, for salad, of course. And finally, the Soup Spot for soup!"

"Have fun!" Sarah and I told them.

For some reason Sarah and I got along best when our parents weren't home. That night, when they left, instead of announcing what we would be doing, she asked me, "What do you want to do?"

I suggested an activity that would make our house look more normal. "Let's prune the jungle," I said. And that's what we did.

The jungle was in our kitchen. Every time someone ate a fruit or vegetable, we planted its seeds. We had grapefruit, avocado, peach, tomato, pepper, pineapple plants, and lots of others. There was just about every kind of fruit and vegetable plant you could think of (except broccoli, of course) all tangled together in the kitchen jungle.

Sarah started trimming the plants on the left side of the kitchen, and I did the ones on the right. By the time we met in the middle, they looked much neater, almost like normal house plants.

Encouraged by our first activity, I asked Sarah, "Do you feel like baking?"

"Sure," she said. She was being so reasonable! She was even willing to do something totally normal, like baking.

We decided to make a cake. I was expecting to have to talk her out of some weird shape, but she got out a regular round cake pan. We set out flour, eggs, butter, baking soda, salt, milk, and vanilla. We mixed them all together.

This was going great! My sister was on the way to being normal. We were cooperating so well that I jumped ahead to the hope of our teaming up to unweird our parents!

We couldn't find one important ingredient for our cake—sugar. We didn't find any honey or molasses either.

"I have a solution!" said Sarah. She ran off on her skinny legs and came back with two chocolate bars she'd been saving since two Halloweens before. Chocolate had lots of sugar, so I figured, why not? We crumbled up the sugar-filled chocolate bars and added the pieces to the batter.

Not long after we got the cake in the oven, the doorbell sounded the first seven notes of "Somewhere Over the Rainbow." It was Patti, stopping by on the way home from her Young Raccoons meeting.

As she joined us in the kitchen, I noticed it was a real mess. Sarah and I had sifted more flour onto the floor than into the mixing bowl. Batter was splattered on the refrigerator, the oven door, the jungle plants, the grand piano, and even in Sarah's bright red hair.

I said something to Patti that I'd heard a soap opera character proclaim on one of her family's TVs: "What must you think of us? This place is a disgrace!"

Patti giggled and said in her little voice, "It's cool city, you guys. Creative cooks are always messy."

"I like the way your bangs are cut," Sarah told Patti. "Your hair is such a pretty blonde." Sarah was actually being polite to my friend!

"*Your* hair is a beautiful red," Patti said to Sarah.

"Thank you," said Sarah. More politeness! "My curls are natural, by the way," she added, as if anyone would *try* to make their hair look like her bird's nest.

We talked for a while about school and other normal (yes, normal!) things.

Suddenly, Patti said she had to go home.

"Can you stay and have some of our cake?" I asked.

"No, my parents eat dinner at exactly six o'clock every night," she said. "They're boring city."

I thought how nice it would be to have a boring but normal family like Patti's. Maybe I *would* have an ordinary family some day—either I would finally unweird my family or I would move in with Patti's.

When Patti left, Sarah took the cake out of the oven and cut two slices. We were really hungry by now. The cake smelled a little funny ...

We each took big bites. Yuck! The cake was disgusting! It didn't even taste like food. Did you ever eat a rubber eraser? I didn't either, but I thought the cake tasted like one.

Sarah and I both spit out our mouthfuls. We groaned and gagged. We drank glass after glass of water to wash away the taste. Then we opened the kitchen windows to get rid of the smell.

"I guess that old Halloween candy wasn't such a good idea," said Sarah. I was pleased to hear her admit she had made a mistake.

"Patti's lucky she didn't stay for the cake," I said.

"You're right," said Sarah and added, "I'm starved."

"Me too." I suggested a normal dinner for two sisters to eat when their parents were out—"How about a pizza?"

Sarah surprised me again by agreeing to my idea. She called the Chesterville House of Pizza and ordered a large pizza because we were so hungry. She ordered plain cheese on my half. On her half, she ordered brussels sprouts and pickles. The person taking the order made her repeat it three times since he thought he'd heard it wrong the first two times.

I didn't comment, figuring I'd work on unweirding her eating habits another time.

While we waited for the pizza delivery, we dropped a piece of the cake in Gomer's bowl. One good thing about Sarah's weirdo pet was that he ate just about anything. But even Gomer didn't seem to want our cake.

"You stubborn urchin!" Sarah said to him.

I'd never heard Sarah give Gomer anything but praise. I jumped at the chance to say, "Maybe we should get a dog for a pet instead."

"If Gomer keeps being such a picky eater, I will consider

it," said Sarah.

I felt more hopeful than ever!

Since Gomer wasn't interested in the cake, we cut it into little pieces and put them outside in our father's coconut shell and soda can birdfeeders. Maybe birds didn't have taste buds.

As we filled the birdfeeders, we noticed that it was really cold for August. It couldn't have been more than 50 degrees.

When we were back inside, the doorbell rang the first seven notes of "Somewhere Over the Rainbow" again.

"Who desires entrance, and what is your purpose?" asked Sarah.

"Pizza delivery," a man's voice said. It was George. We knew him from other times our family had ordered pizza.

Sarah opened the door, and George handed her the box. "I was listening to the radio," he said. "This is the coldest August temperature here in 75 years!"

Sarah and I set out napkins, water glasses and the pizza box. George was still standing near the door. He reminded us the pizza wasn't free.

This was a problem because I didn't have any money. Sarah didn't either. She handed the pizza box back to George. She and I set off on a money hunt, and George sat down on one of the living room mattresses to wait.

We looked for money all over the house—in drawers,

in cabinets, and under beds.

"I found them!" Sarah yelled jubilantly.

I ran into her room to find out how much money she'd come up with. But it turned out she had found her six missing creamed corn labels, in the bottom of a desk drawer.

I peeked in the living room. George had fallen asleep on a living room mattress with the pizza box on his stomach.

Sarah and I searched everywhere we could think of, but we didn't find any money. Even the living room gumball machine was out of pennies.

We woke George up. "I'm sorry, we can't find any money," Sarah told him.

George sat up with a scowl. "I'm tired of kids ordering pizzas delivered to a phony address or not having money to pay," he said.

"I guess you'll have to take the pizza back," said Sarah.

"What good will that do?" grumbled George. "No one else will want pizza with brussels sprouts and pickles."

"That's only on half of it," I muttered.

"We'll pay you later," said Sarah.

"You *better* pay me!" said George. "Get the money to me by eight o'clock tonight, or I'll call the police!"

When he shoved the pizza box into Sarah's hands, I noticed a large grease circle on his stomach where the pizza box had been resting. He stomped out the door muttering, "Crazy kids—arrggh."

I did *not* want George to call the police. For one thing, I didn't want to get in trouble. And I definitely didn't want my sister and me to be in the *Chesterville News* for doing something weird *again*!

I thought of asking Patti to borrow money. But I knew her family was eating dinner, and I didn't want to disturb them, especially if I needed to move in with them some day. I almost called Grant, but then I remembered he was still at summer camp. I considered asking a neighbor, but the neighbors thought we were weird enough already.

Sarah told me not to worry—she would find a way to pay George before eight o'clock. She pulled our father's safari hat over her big red hair to help her think.

I wanted to keep our dinner warm, so I turned on the oven to "warm" and put the pizza box in.

"I've got it!" said Sarah, and she explained her money-making idea. It sounded strange, but we needed to do something fast or we'd be reported to the police. We might even get arrested!

Following Sarah's plan, we pulled all the blankets off her bed, my bed, and our parents' bed, and we took the extra blankets out of the hall closet. We folded them all, then slid them into two plastic garbage bags, adding Sarah's roller skates to one of them.

Each carrying a bag over our shoulders, we set off for the Chesterville Movie Theater.

It was almost time for the 7:30 show of a new movie called *The Two-Hour Minute.*

People waited in a long line to buy tickets.

You could tell that the people in line were cold because a lot of them hopped from one leg to the other.

Sarah laced up her skates and started rolling up and down the sidewalk next to the line. Her big curly red hair shone brightly under the street lights. She shouted: "It's a cold night, everyone! The coldest in 75 years! Get your wool blankets here! Genuine wool blankets! Five dollars apiece!"

She pulled a blanket out of her plastic garbage bag and held it up for the crowd to see. "Doesn't this look warm?" she asked. She draped it over her shoulders saying, "That sure feels good."

"I'll take one," said a shivering man wearing shorts and a tank top. He paid for the blanket and wrapped it around himself.

Then a teenage boy bought one, and he and his date wore it like a big two-person shawl.

Sarah's plan was working out amazingly well. In about three minutes she sold every blanket in her garbage bag. I handed her mine, and she sold the rest of the blankets in the next five minutes.

Now we had money to pay for our pizza! We wouldn't

get arrested, and our names wouldn't be in the newspaper for doing something else weird.

But when I looked at the wad of five-dollar bills in Sarah's hand, I realized something else amazing, but not a good kind of amazing. We had sold all the blankets in the house, but to pay for the pizza, we'd only needed to sell *one*!

When I blurted this out to Sarah, she just said, "Oh, well."

We were freezing and could have used a blanket for ourselves. To warm up, Sarah roller-skated and I jogged next to her all the way to the pizza parlor. George was boxing a pizza behind the counter.

"I told you we'd pay you back," said Sarah, catching her breath. She handed him one of the five-dollar bills.

"Yep. Thanks," said George and slid the money into the cash register.

I wondered if weirdness was contagious. It wasn't like me to go along with Sarah's crazy blanket-selling idea. When George threatened to call the police, I forgot all about my plan to unweird my sister. Instead of my unweirding her, she was making *me* weird.

"Sorry you had to wait for the money," I said to George. I grabbed another five-dollar bill from Sarah and handed it to him.

George nodded at me and smiled, probably not just because of the tip but because he felt sorry that I was stuck in a weirdo family. From all the times he'd delivered pizza to us, he knew about the peculiar things inside and outside our house, even Gomer.

Now George could probably tell that I was getting weird, too. I wondered if he'd noticed the pizza-sized grease circle on his stomach yet.

———————

As soon as Sarah and I opened our front door, I could tell something was wrong. The house smelled terrible, and the air was smoky.

I ran into the kitchen. Smoke was pouring out of the oven. I turned it off and opened the oven door. The pizza box was all black, and it was shooting up smoke.

I knew my parents would be coming home any minute, and my chest felt like the TV from Rent-a-Thing had landed right on it. They would find the kitchen speckled with batter, the house reeking, the air filled with smoke, and we would have to tell them we had sold all the blankets!

Sarah just said, "I'm really starved now. It's too bad the pizza got all dried out." At least she didn't call me a doofus for leaving the oven on. Which I deserved to be called.

Just then our parents walked in. My mother headed for the refrigerator, poured herself a glass of orange juice, and started gargling.

"Your mother has a slight case of indigestion from eating so many different foods and in such large quantities

during our backwards dinner," said my father.

"I feel much better now," my mother said. "Is it kind of smoky in here?"

"The air does seem rather gray," agreed my father, opening a window.

"Oh, Mom and Daddy, I'm so sorry," I said. "I left the oven on and burned the pizza box. And we didn't have any money to pay for the pizza, so we sold all the blankets and ..."

"Slow down," said my father. "What's this about blankets?"

"It's all very logical," said Sarah. As she was telling the story of our evening, we heard a siren. It got louder and louder. Finally, it stopped, and the beginning of "Somewhere Over the Rainbow" sounded for the third time that night, along with pounding on the door.

"Who could that be?" said my mother.

We all went to the door, where there were two fire fighters. One held a hose, and one clutched an axe. "Where's the fire?" the one with the hose shouted as they rushed into the living room.

"Oh, there's no fire," said my father.

"Well, someone, I think Snooterman was his name, reported smoke coming out of your kitchen window," the fire fighter with the axe said. "It certainly *smells* like smoke in here!"

"Everything is under control now," said my mother. "You see, the kids ordered a half cheese, half brussels sprouts-and-pickles pizza ..."

Why did my mother have to be so honest? She told the fire fighters every detail of our weird evening, from our using old Halloween candy to sweeten a cake, to her new plan to keep a ten-dollar bill in our encyclopedia under "money" in case Sarah and I needed cash in a hurry again.

The fire fighters kept looking at each other with wide eyes. Towards the end of my mother's tale, they sat down on mattresses. They must have been tired of standing there listening and holding their heavy equipment.

"Well, young lady," the fire fighter with the axe said to me. "I guess you know now not to do something weird like leaving a cardboard box in a warm oven."

I nodded. The word "weird" smarted like a bee sting.

Since we had wasted the fire fighters' time, my mother signed them up for ten free fencing lessons each.

After they left, I apologized again to my parents for the trouble I'd caused.

"It's OK," said my mother. "I'm sure you learned your lesson about putting anything flammable in the oven. And you were both very clever to find a way to make money."

"Yes, you were highly imaginative," said my father.

"You're not angry with us for selling all the blankets?" asked Sarah.

"Of course not, Cindy Toucan and Sarah Butterfly," said my father. "I know how it is to get carried away once in a while. We'll use sleeping bags tonight, and we'll buy new blankets tomorrow. The leftover money you made from selling the old blankets should pay for one or two new ones."

"What about the sticky mess in the kitchen?" I asked.

"We'll clean it up together," said my mother brightly. "We're just glad you didn't start a serious fire and get hurt. Right, Smith?"

"Absolutely!" said my father. "And we're pleased that you girls had fun together." He twirled me around in a circle three times and then twirled Sarah three times.

I had to admit to myself that I did have fun with Sarah that night ... most of the time.

Sarah gave Gomer a piece of the burnt pizza. He must have liked it better than our cake because it disappeared in a couple of minutes. "That reminds me," said Sarah. "I'm starved."

"I'm so starved!" I said.

Luckily, my parents had gotten full after the first four courses of their backwards dinner and couldn't eat one spoonful of their soup. They had brought it home, so Sarah and I got to enjoy delicious tomato soup and chicken noodle soup. As I wolfed down two bowls, I thought about the advantages of having weirdos for parents.

A lot of parents would yell if you did the foolish things Sarah and I had done. But weird parents didn't mind if *you* did something weird.

That's when it hit me—I was *definitely* getting weird. Putting chocolate bars in cake batter, ordering pizza without having money, selling blankets ... Even the fire fighter said leaving a pizza box in the oven was a weird thing to do.

My one-at-a-time unweirding plan hadn't worked with my mother, my father, *or* my sister. It was just a matter of time before I was as weird as the rest of the Krinkles. I had done so many weird things in one night. Soon I would be twirling a baton on a skateboard and collecting different color tissue boxes!

Maybe I should move in with Patti before it's too late, I thought.

7

An Evening with Unweirdos

About a week after school started, Patti invited me over for dinner. We hadn't gotten to spend as much time together as the year before because we were in different fifth-grade classes. I was in Mrs. Reed's class again. (Mrs. Reed moved up to fifth grade from fourth grade, like me.) But Patti was in Mr. Howard's class.

All day I looked forward to spending an evening with unweirdos. School was horrendous because Mrs. Reed had told us to write a composition about something interesting we had done over the weekend.

I hated assignments like "What I Did Over the Weekend" or "My Summer Vacation." I could never think of anything to write about because everything my family did was weird. I could have titled my compositions "What the Weirdos Did on their Very Weird Vacation" or "Help! I'm a Prisoner in a Weird Family."

Staring at my blank paper, I thought about what we'd done over the weekend—we moved some of our outdoor weeds to the kitchen jungle, we played the pretend orchestra game, and we had a beginning-of-the-school-year party for my mother's fencing students. Everything seemed too oddball-ish to write about.

Eventually, I wrote about painting a new mural on the living room wall. My mother wanted fresh artwork for the fencing students party. And after I practiced piano, I didn't have anything better to do, so I painted, too.

We started with white paint to cover the mural we had created with Marguerite. While it was drying, we decided that our new mural would show our favorite foods. Sarah painted a brussels sprouts-and-pickles pizza. My mother painted her dream—a drinking fountain that spouted orange juice. My father painted *his* favorite, rice with chocolate sauce. I painted a hamburger and French fries.

What I hadn't realized was that Mrs. Reed would make us read our compositions out loud. She had never done anything like that the year before. She used to be so nice!

When we finished writing, Mrs. Reed announced: "Now we will share some of your compositions. It will be good practice to read out loud. And it will help you get to know each other since you weren't all in the same class last year."

If I had known about this sharing with the class deal, I wouldn't have written about painting on the living room wall. I would have said my family watched a baseball game on TV. Actually, I wouldn't have written that. My family didn't watch baseball, we didn't own a TV, and I didn't like to lie.

Tapping my feet under my desk, I thought, *Don't call on me, don't call on me.*

"Cindy, how about you?" asked Mrs. Reed with a smile.

I know I just said I didn't like to lie, but this was an emergency! I pointed at my throat and whispered, "Sorry, Mrs. Reed. I have laryngitis." I hoped I looked pale and sick. Judging by the way my face felt though, it was probably as bright red as Sarah's hair. Maybe Mrs. Reed would think I was flushed with a fever.

"I'm sorry you're sick," said Mrs. Reed, looking concerned.

It worked!

"Since you have laryngitis, Cindy, I'll read your essay to the class," Mrs. Reed horrified me by saying.

There was no way out. Looking down at the scuffed-with-kids'-feet classroom floor, I handed her my essay. As she read it, loudly and clearly, I actually did feel sick. *That'll teach you not to lie*, I thought.

Everybody in my class heard about my family's tradition of painting on the living room wall.

At the end, Brenda, who was in my class three years in a row, called out, "Those are the strangest food combinations I've ever heard! And who paints on their wall?"

"The Krinkles' murals are really cool," said Grant. "I wish *my* family would do stuff like that."

"Me too!" said a girl named Molly.

Other kids read essays about normal things their families had done over the weekend. Brenda read about bowling. Karen described visiting a whaling museum. Seth actually *volunteered* to read his essay. He and his family had gone to his cousin's wedding, and he got to stay up until midnight.

To make things worse, Mrs. Reed knelt down at my desk and asked softly if I wanted to go to the nurse.

Since I was supposed to have laryngitis, I just shook my head. I felt bad that I had lied to my kind teacher.

————————

During lunch, Grant told me he was relieved that Mrs. Reed hadn't called on him.

"Why?" I asked, leaving most of my inside-out peanut butter and jelly sandwich untouched.

Grant didn't say anything about my sudden ability to talk. I figured he understood why. "My family did something really embarrassing over the weekend," he said quietly. "But it was the only thing I could think of to write about."

I didn't bug him to tell me what his family had done, but I was curious.

"I'll tell you if you promise not to tell anyone,"

offered Grant.

"I promise."

"Well," said Grant, the noise of the lunch room keeping other kids from hearing, "my mother's boss came over for dinner, and she was super nervous. Everything went fine until dessert, when she accidentally spilled coffee on the boss's jacket. Then she was so busy trying to clean his jacket that she forgot she had started running water for my little brother's bath upstairs. It overflowed out the bathroom, down the stairs, and all the way into the living room! Her boss ended up having to help mop up the mess."

"Oh no!" I said. "Your poor mom!"

"My little brother thought the whole thing was awesome. You should have seen him jumping in the living room puddles!" Grant was smiling now.

"Ha! I can picture him! By the way, Grant, thanks for saying our living room murals are cool."

"They are!"

That night at Patti's, I wasn't in the mood for being embarrassed further. I wanted her parents to like me in case my family proved impossible to unweird or I found *myself* starting to turn weird. In either case, I would need to ask them if I could move in.

I made sure to show up at Patti's house right before six o'clock, when her family always ate.

"Nice to see you, Cindy!" said her father with a wide smile.

"Come in! I hope you brought your appetite," said Patti's mother, hugging me— not a bear hug like my mother's—just a normal one.

So far, so good, I thought.

We sat down at the kitchen table. Patti's father had to sit kind of far from the table because he had a big stomach. You could tell he didn't ride a bike to work or do cartwheels around the house. You could tell he rode in a golf cart or had someone else carry his clubs when he played.

We all had our own plates, not like in my house, where we ate out of one pot.

Patti's father turned on the TV in the kitchen. I knew there was another TV in the family room and another in the master bedroom. I was surprised that they watched TV during dinner. Usually, I went to Patti's right after school, and I went home before dinnertime.

A news show was on.

We each ate half a grapefruit. I was very careful not to squirt anyone.

Everybody was quiet. I thought her parents might be avoiding a conversation with me because they suddenly remembered Marguerite's article in the *Chesterville News*. Or maybe when Roger Snooterman delivered their paper, he told them stories about the Krinkles. Maybe they just didn't feel like talking to a kid from a weirdo family.

I figured I should start a conversation to show them I wasn't so bad. "This grapefruit is delicious!" I said.

"Ssh!" said Patti's father. He had been so friendly at first, but now he didn't seem to want anything to do with me. I figured he was angry with Patti for inviting me in the first place. And she had said they wouldn't mind if I moved in!

When a commercial came on, Patti's father turned to me and asked, "How do you like being in the Young Blue Jays, Cindy?"

I told him I liked it and that my group had gone on a field trip to a fish hatchery over the summer.

"That must have been interesting," said Patti's mother. She cleared away the grapefruit plates and took out a salad bowl and salad plates from a cabinet. Patti's family sure used a lot of plates.

I asked Patti's mother if I could help her carry something. Just then the commercial ended.

"Ssh!" her father said again. And everybody got quiet. Then I caught on—they talked only during commercials.

When the next commercial came on, Patti's father told me about a fish hatchery he had once visited. During the commercial after that, Patti's mother said that fish had gotten very expensive.

Except for grapefruit and salad, I had never eaten any of the foods we had that night. We ate fried chicken Patti's mother had bought frozen in a box, peas and corn from another frozen box, and pound cake from a box. Everything was delicious.

I thought how nice it would be to eat from my very own plate at dinner and to know that I had to listen to Sarah only during commercials.

I thought it would be nice to know that dinner would always be ready at exactly six o'clock.

The best part would be living with a family I wouldn't feel embarrassed by.

After dinner I made sure to help clear the table and clean up the kitchen, which took more time than at my house because of all the plates. Then her parents watched more TV, on the TV in the family room, and Patti and I went up to her room.

For such a small person, Patti had a really big room. It used to be her sister's before she got married. The smaller bedroom used to be Patti's. That would be mine if I moved in. I peeked in, and it looked very comfy. No can labels on the walls. No bowl with a sea urchin.

"It must be great to live in a normal household," I said plopping next to her on her bed.

"It's pretty dull city," said Patti. "Everything's always the same. Dinner at six, TV always on. Every Friday my mother goes to the hairdresser. Every Saturday during good weather, my father plays golf. In bad weather, he watches golf on TV."

"I would like always knowing what would happen," I said. "I'm tired of weird surprises."

"When my big sister was here, things were a little livelier," said Patti. "At least she used to pick on me, and we would fight once in a while."

"I wouldn't miss fighting with Sarah."

"It's too bad you don't realize how fabulous your family is," said Patti. "But if you're really unhappy, I'll talk to my parents about your moving in. I would love it! You and I would have a blast!"

"Well ..." I said.

Just then we heard the doorbell. It didn't play a tune, like the doorbell at my house. It just went "ding dong."

"Patti!" called her father. "Aunt Luba is here. Put on your tap shoes!"

"Oh, sugar," Patti muttered. "Sugar, salt and pepper!" She didn't move from her bed.

"Patti!" her father called up the stairs again.

"Dad, I don't feel like it!" she yelled as loudly as her little voice would go.

"You have two minutes to get down here!" her father announced. "Aunt Luba came especially to see the new dance you learned."

With a sigh, Patti got up and pulled a pair of tap shoes out of her closet. She jammed them onto her little feet.

81

"I didn't know you could tap-dance," I said, surprised not to know something about my best friend.

"Well, now you know," she muttered.

"How did you learn?"

"My parents *make* me take lessons."

I followed her down to the living room. Her mother turned on music and sat on the couch between Patti's father and Aunt Luba. The three of them folded their hands across their stomachs.

Hunched over and scowling, Patti stood on the flagstones in front of the fireplace.

"We're waiting, little Patti," said Aunt Luba.

Patti began to tap-dance, her short blonde hair bouncing up and down. She danced really, really well, and the taps sounded cool on the flagstones. But I could tell she hated tap dancing.

"Smile, Patti!" said Aunt Luba. So Patti danced with this phony-looking smile that had a frown underneath.

Afterwards, everyone clapped.

"You dance like a professional, Patti!" said Aunt Luba.

"Doesn't she?" said Patti's mother, beaming.

Back up in her room, Patti yanked off her tap shoes and flung them into her closet. She slammed the closet door shut.

"You were incredible!" I said.

"Too bad," said Patti. "If my parents thought I had no

talent, they would let me quit."

"Why do they make you take lessons if you don't like them?"

"Because my father wanted to take lessons when *he* was a kid," said Patti. "But his parents couldn't afford them."

"What does that have to do with you?"

Patti shrugged. "The worst part is they always make me dance in front of relatives. It's so embarrassing!"

Patti didn't seem to feel like doing any more talking. So I patted her shoulder, said good-bye and went downstairs to thank her parents for dinner.

On my way out, I heard her father say, "That Cindy is a good kid."

As I walked home, I thought how Patti's normal, totally unweird parents were surprisingly embarrassing. I also thought how I would miss my family if I didn't live with them.

Maybe moving in with Patti *wasn't* the answer.

Then I remembered that Grant's mother had embarrassed him when her boss came for dinner.

It seemed that my family wasn't the only embarrassing one around. At least they didn't make me take lessons I hated or tap-dance for relatives. They didn't yell at me for selling all our blankets and almost starting a fire either.

But when I reached my driveway, I heard the raucous sounds of the nightly screaming session. Instead of going inside, I paced around the rocket ship and penguin-shaped bushes until the screams stopped.

Maybe other people's families were embarrassing sometimes. But I was sure no one's was as mortifying as mine —all the time! I was sick of having only weird things to write about at school. I was tired of hiding in the closet when Roger Snooterman came to the door to get paid for delivering the paper.

I made up my mind. I would try one more unweirding plan. I promised myself it would be the last one. If it didn't work ... well ... I didn't want to move in with Patti anymore ... so it just *had* to work!

8

~~~~~~

One Last Chance

My next and final unweirding plan struck me as foolproof. The leader of my Young Blue Jays group was out of town and couldn't be in charge of our next field trip. So I asked my parents to lead us on the hike up Tulip Mountain.

Of course, they said yes. Sarah said she would come, too.

I had told my family so much about the Young Blue Jays that I thought they might have some idea how to act around them. But, following my foolproof plan, I had my parents and sister read all the rules of behavior in the Young Blue Jays Handbook. I even gave them a quiz, and they did great! That meant they were very likely to follow the rules the whole day of the hike. And they would have so much fun acting normal, for a change, they would volunteer to unweird themselves forever after! Even Roger Snooterman would notice the difference.

The plan was a tiny bit risky—if Sarah and my parents

acted weird despite all my preparation, the Young Blue Jays would find out just how weird they were. They might even throw me out of the group. But it was a chance I had to take if I was ever going to unweird the Weirdos.

The morning of the hike, I asked my mother if she would try to act normal all day, at least while the Young Blue Jays were around.

"Who?" she asked.

"The Young Blue Jays. Our hike is today!"

"Oh, yes, I'm looking forward to it!" she said.

"Well, will you?" I asked.

"Will I what?"

"Will you act normal?"

"Of course, Cindy. I'll act the same as always."

Just then my plan didn't seem so foolproof. My stomach felt like a swarm of bumblebees had gotten in it somehow. While Sarah and my parents got dressed (I had been dressed for hours), I went into the kitchen and played the grand piano to calm myself down.

The doorbell rang the first seven notes of "Somewhere Over the Rainbow."

I made my way to the door so slowly that the seven notes played again.

"What a funny doorbell!" the Young Blue Jay at the door said. The bees in my stomach started buzzing more.

One by one, the Blue Jays rang the bell and, for the first

time, entered the headquarters of the Weirdos.

There were eight Young Blue Jays. There was only one of me. More than ever, I wished Patti had joined my group instead of the Young Raccoons.

In the living room, the Blue Jays pointed things out to each other—the gumball machine, the mural of different foods, the water fountain—why hadn't I suggested we meet at the Tulip Mountain parking lot instead of my house?

"What's this?" asked one of the Blue Jays.

"That's Gomer, my sister's pet sea urchin," I mumbled.

Just then Sarah whooshed into the room. She was wearing her karate suit for the hike. And she was carrying her baton.

"Hi Sarah," said a Young Blue Jay who lived in our neighborhood.

Sarah didn't answer. She fed Gomer some of her leftover breakfast—split-pea soup. Yes, split-pea soup. For breakfast.

"Hey Sarah," another Blue Jay said. Sarah still didn't answer.

"Sarah!" I hissed. "Remember the handbook rules? You're supposed to be polite."

Finally, my sister turned to the Blue Jays and announced: "My name is not Sarah. I have changed my name to Ethel."

"Since when?" I yelped.

"Since this morning." She looked ridiculously proud of

herself. I wished she would stay home and read the D's in the dictionary instead of coming along to ruin the hike.

I ran to find my mother, who was wrapping sandwiches in the kitchen. At least she'd remembered to make lunches.

"Mom, why did you let Sarah change her name to Ethel?"

"Why wouldn't I?" was her answer.

"Because it's weird to change her name, especially to Ethel."

"Whatever she wants to be called is fine with your father and me. After all, I changed *my* name from Crystal to Squirrel."

"But Sarah's still a child." I tried to keep my voice down so the Young Blue Jays wouldn't hear. "She's too young to change her name. How would you like it if I changed *my* name to ... to ... Caboose?"

"That would be fun!" said my mother, chuckling at the thought.

There was no use talking to her. I stomped out of the kitchen.

Back in the living room, my father was showing the Blue Jays his watercolor tattoos. In honor of the hike, he had painted a blue jay on one arm and an ostrich on the other.

"We won't see ostriches on our hike, will we, Mr. Krinkle?" asked one of the girls.

"No," said my father. "But I am extremely fond of ostriches."

"I'd like to paint tattoos on my arms," said one of the Blue Jays.

"Me too," several others said.

"The next time I have the privilege of hosting one of your meetings, I will be pleased to show you how," said my father, who already did look pleased.

I could just imagine the reactions of the Young Blue Jays' parents if their daughters came home with tattoos. I'd get kicked out of the group, for sure.

We all piled into the flowers-and-robots-painted van. Actually, not all of us. My father rode next to the van on his bicycle. Since it was sunny, he had the umbrella open.

In the center of Chesterville, a police officer was directing traffic. My father rode right near him and beeped the first four notes of "Frère Jacques" on his bicycle horn. The police officer jumped about six inches.

"Just saying hello!" called my father, tipping his safari hat.

"The Blue Jays guffawed and said, "Did you see the cop jump?"

I didn't find this funny at all. I thought you could even get arrested for scaring a police officer. Apparently, the officer already knew my umbrella-bike-riding, opera singing father. He smiled and said, "You got me, Smith!"

At Tulip Mountain, we parked near the beginning of a trail. My father locked his bike to a tree, and we set off on the hike. Being active made the bumblebees in my stomach quiet down.

Sarah (or rather, Ethel) twirled her baton while she walked. My father picked dandelions and made necklaces out of them for the Blue Jays. I tossed mine away. I did not feel like wearing a weed necklace.

After a while, we came to a cleared, level spot and stopped for lunch. My mother unpacked the food—grape juice boxes, apples, and peanut-butter-and-jelly sandwiches with the bread on the inside—in air-sickness bags. At the sight of those bags I did feel air-sick, or ground-sick.

At least my mother had brought lots of napkins for the inside-out peanut-butter-and-jelly sandwiches.

Sarah (or rather, Ethel) was the only person in the world who didn't like jelly. So my mother had made her a peanut-butter-and-pickles sandwich.

One of the Young Blue Jays opened her backpack and pulled out her handbook. Looking over the chapter about hikes, she asked my father why he was wearing short sleeves. The handbook said you should wear long sleeves on hikes to avoid insect bites.

"I have my own methods," said my father. "Before we left, I rubbed my arms with onions to keep bugs away. That was before I painted on the tattoos, of course."

The Blue Jays giggled. They probably thought he was kidding about the onions.

Now the Blue Jay with the handbook asked my mother why she was wearing sneakers. The chapter about hikes said you're supposed to wear sturdy shoes.

"Oh, I know," said my mother with a smile, "but I'd go crazy without my red sneakers." She looked pretty crazy as it was, with her wild gray hair, pink warm-up suit, neon green socks, and red sneakers. At least she wasn't wearing her tutu.

Of course, Ethel had to start carrying on about her dumb collection. "I have seven hundred and seventy-four can labels in my room, including 84 creamed corn labels," she announced, as if this was something to be enormously proud of.

"That's a lot of labels!" said one of the Blue Jays.

"Wow!" another Blue Jay said.

I was sure they were trying to be polite, according to the rule in The Young Blue Jays Handbook. All the Blue Jays told my mother that the lunch was delicious, too.

We packed our trash in our backpacks and started climbing again.

"I asked *my* parents to take our group on a hike," said one of the Blue Jays. "My mother said she had to play bridge, and my father said he has to take it easy on Saturdays because he works hard all week."

"I asked my parents, too," another Blue Jay said. "But they were going to a wedding."

The next part of the path was steeper. When we got to some benches made out of logs, we took a rest break.

Suddenly, my mother jumped up from her log and asked, "Who would like to hear bird call imitations?"

Before anyone answered, she scrambled up a tree, like her name, Squirrel. My father followed. They found a branch to sit on, and the concert began.

Right then I wished *my* parents had been too busy to take us on the hike.

The Blue Jays looked up in the tree and cheered for the imitations, which sounded like real bird calls. Maybe I would have cheered too, if the two grown-ups chirping and whistling on a tree branch weren't my parents. But they were.

After our break, it didn't take long to climb the last part of the trail. There was just one more steep section, and we were at a clearing on top of the mountain.

"We made it!" the Blue Jays shouted.

The view was amazing. We could see far off in the distance to other mountains. In the valley below we saw a pond, fields with cows, buildings in Chesterville, and cars driving along roads. Everything looked so tiny.

But that's when my plan, even after my family had read

the handbook rules and gotten excellent scores on my quiz, totally fell apart. The handbook said when you were out in nature, you should keep your voices down. My family raised their voices instead.

Ethel twirled her baton while chanting a victory cheer:

"Mom drove us, Daddy-Cakes biked.

Then up up up up up we hiked.

Who are the greatest hikers today?

We all know—it's the Young Blue Jays!"

When she chanted it again, everyone joined in, except me.

My mother celebrated our climb by doing cartwheels.

My father bellowed a song from an Italian opera, leaning his head back and gazing up at the sky. That made his safari hat fall off, and you could see the bald top of his head above his long hair. His performance would have been slightly less embarrassing if he sang on key.

I couldn't take all this weirdness anymore. I walked away.

I kept walking until I heard the opera singing only faintly. I sank down and slumped against a tree.

My family's weird behavior had completely spoiled the hike. The Young Blue Jays were too polite to show they were as exasperated as I was, but I was sure they were. They would end up asking me to leave the group, and I wouldn't blame them.

I was so disappointed. My so-called foolproof unweirding plan was a disaster. And it was my family's last chance!

Then I noticed that the opera singing had stopped. So had the cheers, whoops, and chants. I hurried back to the clearing. There was no one there.

The Young Blue Jays and my family had headed down the mountain without me.

I was all by myself on top of the mountain.

9

Weirdos to the Rescue

Maybe I can still catch up with them, I thought. But I
didn't see how.

There were five different trails. My family and the Blue
Jays might have taken any one of them.

I ran along the beginning of each trail, yelling, "Mom-
mmm! Daddee! Blue Jays!" But there was no answer.

"Ethel!" Still no answer.

My father once told me that if I ever got lost, I should
find a security guard or stay in one place and wait. There
was no security guard on the mountain. No lifeguard with
a bullhorn either. So I climbed onto a big rock and waited.
And waited.

I could tell it would get dark in about an hour. If my
parents didn't notice I was missing until they got home,
they wouldn't even *start* looking for me until after dark. I
hated the dark. I always slept with a night light. Even if I'd

brought a night light in my backpack, there was no place on top of Tulip Mountain to plug it in.

I wondered if there were grizzly bears living on the mountain. Or bats?

Grant, Patti, and I once watched a movie that had a really scary part with bats. Kids trapped in a cave were attacked by a shrieking, flying mob of them. Waiting all alone on the rock, I kept picturing that mob of bats.

Then I heard a real shriek. "Eeek!" It was me.

Don't think about bats, I thought.

On top of the mountain it was really quiet. Too quiet. I could hear every leaf flutter, every bird peep. The fluttering of leaves sounded like a hungry grizzly bear approaching. Birds flying overhead looked like bats ready to dive down on me.

Don't think about bats.

Don't think about grizzly bears.

The breeze got stronger. I pulled my hat lower on my head. All I had on over my T-shirt was a light jacket. The Blue Jays Handbook warned that it got cold on mountains at night. I did *not* want to freeze to death.

Think of something pleasant, I told myself.

I thought how glad I would be when my parents showed up. They just *had* to show up.

But the happiness of picturing my parents rescuing me disappeared when I remembered I would have to face the Young Blue Jays afterwards. Nothing good was in store for me at the bottom of the mountain—just more embarrassment and getting kicked out of the Blue Jays. I was terrified of what would happen to me on top of the mountain and dreading what would happen on the bottom.

Then I heard a loud rustling of leaves. My parents? I looked over to where the crunchy sound was coming from and saw a black and white animal the size of a dachshund. It was a skunk.

The skunk was headed towards my rock.

It stopped moving when it saw me, or smelled me, or heard my heart pounding. It raised itself up and seemed to stare at me. I stared at it.

Please don't spray me, I thought.

I knew that skunks sprayed when they felt threatened. I sat very still so it wouldn't think I was dangerous. Trying to look friendly, I smiled at the skunk. It didn't smile back.

This is the worst, I thought. There I was, alone on top of a rock, on top of a mountain—cold, scared, mortified. And instead of my parents finding me, a skunk did! Roger Snooterman would have laughed himself silly to see me up on a rock, grinning at a skunk.

I was worried enough that people wouldn't like me because I had a weird family. Now I had a new worry—if I got sprayed, everyone would call me Skunky.

I thought about the time Grant's dog got sprayed by a

skunk. After a whole week and 14 tomato juice baths, he still smelled like a skunk.

Then I remembered reading in the handbook that some animals thought you were a threat if you stared at them. So I stopped smiling at the skunk. I stopped looking at it altogether. I curled up on the rock and closed my eyes, hoping the skunk would think I was asleep and wander away.

The rock was not a comfortable place to curl up at all.

I heard leaves rustling again. *Oh, please, don't spray me,* I thought.

I pretended to be asleep on that hard rock for ages. Every minute or two, I heard the skunk, and my heart felt as if it would thump out of my chest.

The rock felt so cold and rough through my thin jacket and T-shirt. When would my parents come back? Today? *Tomorrow?* Even if they showed up soon, I thought, they might not notice the skunk. If they startled it by mistake, all of us would get sprayed.

After ages and ages, I decided no one was coming, not before dark anyway. But I could still hear the skunk moving around, so I stayed on the rock, rolled up into a ball, shivering and pretending to be asleep.

Please don't spray me, skunk, I kept thinking. *Please come rescue me, Mom and Daddy. Or Sarah. Or Ethel. Someone!*

Then the rustling came closer. And closer! Something wet was on my cheek. "*Aaacchh!*" I screamed.

I tried to keep my eyes closed, but I couldn't.

"Mom!"

"Oh, my Cindy," my mother said wrapping me in a bear hug. "Were you taking a little nap?"

"A nap? No," I wasn't sleeping. I was trying to fool the—aaacchh!!—did you see the skunk?"

"Yes!" said my mother. "Your father and I got it to leave."

"How?" My heart was still pounding about a thousand times a minute.

Helping me down from the rock, my mother said: "We brought some popcorn in case you were hungry when we found you. Ethel and the Young Blue Jays made it in the picnic area fire pit at the bottom of the mountain."

"But what about the skunk, Mom?"

"Yes, the skunk ... well, when we were giving out the popcorn, we noticed you were missing. Your father and I climbed back up the mountain as fast as we could, and we saw that skunk. We stayed very quiet, and we dropped a trail of popcorn leading from the skunk into the woods. The skunk ate the trail and disappeared!"

Just then my father burst out of the woods and said, "The skunk is gone. I'm so glad to see you, Cindy Toucan!" He twirled me around three times.

"I'm sure glad to see you and Mom," I said. Suddenly, I felt so relieved that I wouldn't have to spend the night on the mountain with bats, a grizzly bear, or a skunk that

100

I started to cry. I'd heard that people cry from happiness, but it had never happened to me before.

When my parents saw me crying, they both started crying, too. The three of us hugged in kind of a hug sandwich.

Smack in the warm middle of the hug sandwich, I remembered how much I loved my parents. Yes, they were weird, but they were the kindest people you'd ever want to meet. They wouldn't even hurt a head of broccoli. Or a dandelion.

"I'm so sorry we left you behind," my father said through his tears.

"We thought you were with us," said my mother and blew her nose with a big honk.

"I know you didn't leave me on purpose," I said. "It's my fault for walking away from the group."

"Why did you?" asked my mother.

I didn't want to tell them I was trying to escape from their weirdness. Not when they had just climbed a mountain twice and rescued me from a skunk. They were there when I needed them, just as they always were.

"I had some things to think about," I said.

I *still* had things to think about. As we walked, or rather, jogged, down the mountain, I kept thinking about the Young Blue Jays waiting at the bottom. I pictured them down there, bored and impatient, and ready to kick me out of the group.

My father picked me up on his shoulders and gave me a ride the rest of the way down the mountain.

The closer we came to the bottom, the more panicky I got about seeing the Blue Jays. I was sure they would kick me out. Not only had they had the whole day to see how weird my family was, but *I* had wandered away—like a weirdo.

———————

By the time we reached the bottom of the mountain, it was getting dark. In the picnic area, Ethel and the Blue Jays were sitting in a circle. They all wore the dandelion necklaces my father had made. Ethel was explaining the best way to take a label off a can without tearing it.

"Yay! You found Cindy!" everyone cheered.

As my father let me down from his shoulders, the bumblebees in my stomach woke up. The bumblebees and I waited for someone to say, "We're sorry, Cindy. There's a new rule: no weirdos in the Young Blue Jays."

But first, the Blue Jays and even Ethel wanted to hear about my adventures on top of the mountain. I told them about being cold and frightened. I told them about thinking I heard grizzly bears and bats and then encountering a skunk instead.

"Oh nooooo!" the girls said.

I explained how my parents got the skunk to leave.

"Everything is OK now that you're back," one of the

Blue Jays said.

Now they'll break it to me that instead of the Young Blue Jays, I should be in the Young Cuckoos.

"Cindy, you were a genius to ask your family to take us on a hike!" said one of the Blue Jays. "This has been our best hike ever!"

"What?" I said. Maybe I misunderstood what she said.

"This has been a fantastic day," she went on, "except that you got left behind, of course."

The Blue Jays all started talking at once: "It's been awesome! Yeah! I even liked your father's opera singing. I wish *my* mother could do cartwheels. And your parents' bird calls sounded exactly like birds. Your parents are so unusual and so nice! And Sarah's—I mean Ethel's—baton twirling is amazing!"

I *wasn't* hearing things. The Young Blue Jays liked my family. They appreciated my family! They weren't just being polite.

The girls couldn't stop talking about how much fun they'd had. "Peanut butter and jelly sandwiches taste so much better with the peanut butter and jelly on the outside. And don't you love these dandelion necklaces?"

Patti had been right all along. People thought my family was great, not just weird.

As you can imagine, I felt pretty great hearing the Young Blue Jays rave about the hike with my family. And I realized something fabulous—I didn't have to worry any-more about what the Young Blue Jays or even Roger Snooterman thought of the Krinkles! I wouldn't have to be embarrassed when my parents or sister did something embarrassing around them—because I wouldn't think it was embarrassing. Maybe I could enjoy my family again ...

"We should get going," said my mother. "I can tell by my stomach that it's dinnertime."

"Can we stay here a little longer?" one of the Blue Jays asked. "Our parents know we might be home late."

"Sure," my mother said with a smile. She scooped up a handful of popcorn to hold her over until dinner and gave me some, too.

The girls moved apart to make room for my parents and me to join their circle.

The circle gave me an idea. "Let's play the pretend or-chestra game! It's a game only my family plays," I told the girls.

Ethel turned on the radio in the flowers-and-robots van so we could hear music in the picnic area. When she got back to the circle, she sat next to me and gave me a hug!

I decided that Ethel, or Sarah, or whatever her name was, had her good points. "Thanks for entertaining the girls while Mom and Daddy were looking for me," I whispered.

Since the Young Blue Jays had never played the pretend orchestra game before, I explained how it worked. Then we got started. We listened to the music and moved our hands and mouths as if we were playing different instruments. My mother pretended to play a tuba. My father pretended to play a bassoon. Ethel pretended to play a bass drum. The Blue Jays pretended to play a violin, a clarinet, a flute, a trumpet, a cello, a xylophone, a saxophone, and a harp.

Ethel let me borrow her baton. I was the conductor.

It was super fun.

I felt proud to be part of such a weird, wonderful family.

10

Trick or Treat with the Weirdos

After the young Blue Jays hike, I felt a lot better about things. I hadn't unweirded my family, but I'd found out I didn't have to. Or even want to.

Take Halloween, for instance. My parents did a lot of stuff I *could* have been embarrassed by ...

First of all, there were the treats my mother gave out. She filled air-sickness bags with two pieces of bubble gum from our living room gumball machine, three home-baked porcupine cookies, and a paperback book. "Food for thought," she explained.

Sarah, who fortunately had changed her name back from Ethel, said: "Mom, you're not supposed to give out unwrapped gum or cookies. I heard it on the radio. Kids are warned not to eat anything that didn't come from a store, still in its wrapping."

"Oh," said my mother. She wrote on the outside of each

air-sickness bag: "No poison in here. Guaranteed safe and delicious treats from Squirrel Krinkle, 75 Ash Street, Chestervillle."

"That ought to do the trick," she said. "The trick for the treats!"

While my mother gave out bags to the little kids who came early, I got dressed. Patti and I were going trick-or-treating together.

I had made my own costume. On an old gray shirt and old gray sweatpants I'd painted rows of white squares that were supposed to be windows. I had cut eye, nose, and mouth holes in a paper bag. Then I taped a long piece of a coat hanger to the top of the bag. It shot straight up into the air when I put the paper bag over my head, to look like a spire.

With my costume on, I waited for Patti in the living room. I was careful to keep my arms straight at my sides.

"What are you supposed to be?" asked Sarah folding her skinny arms across her chest and squinting at me.

"A skyscraper."

"Not bad," she said, which was pretty enthusiastic for Sarah to say about something I made.

"I remember this house!" a little kid at the door said. "You gave out inside-out grilled cheese sandwiches last Halloween."

"We sure did!" said my mother, handing him an air-sickness bag. "This year we have different treats. Have fun!"

When Patti showed up, she and I started laughing. We both looked so funny!

Patti was wearing a great costume—a huge cardboard box covered with wrapping paper. She had tied a ribbon in a big bow on top of her blonde head. On the front of the cardboard, she had written, "Surprise!" She was a surprise package.

"Outstanding costume!" said Sarah.

"Are you coming trick-or-treating with us?" Patti asked her.

It wouldn't have taken my sister long to get ready. With her karate suit, baton, and bird's nest hair, she *always* seemed to be wearing a costume. But she said, "I have outgrown Halloween. And besides, I have more important things to do."

She's probably going to clean Gomer's bowl, I thought.

Patti and I were about to leave when someone wearing purple beads, a rubber ape mask, and a white airplane-cleaning uniform skidded into the living room. You guessed it: my father.

He tripped on the edge of one of the living room mattresses and landed on his back on another one. As he picked himself up, he grunted like an ape.

Patti giggled at the sight. "Are you trick-or-treating with us, Mr. Krinkle?" she asked.

"Yes, I have decided to accompany you!" said my father. "I have not gone trick-or-treating in approximately 30 years. And since Cindy's mother always serves healthy food, I would love some perfectly unhealthy candy!" He held up a polka dot tote bag that was apparently for his treats.

If it had been a few weeks earlier, I would have been totally embarrassed by my father wearing a costume and trick-or-treating with us around our neighborhood. But now I thought it was OK.

Besides, it was Halloween. I loved Halloween—*everybody* was weird on Halloween!

"Let's hit the streets!" I said.

We started next door, at the Armstrongs' house.

"Trick or treat!" Patti called in her little voice as she rang the doorbell.

"Trick or treat!" repeated my father in an ape-like grunt.

Mrs. Armstrong came to the door. "I know that's you, Cindy," she said, smiling. "I can tell by your nose freckles peeking out the hole. And I know that's you, little Patti. But who's the tall one in the ape mask with the long black wig?"

"It's me, Smith," grunted my father, "and it's not a wig."

"Oh, of course," said Mrs. Armstrong. She handed candy bars to Patti and me.

"What about me?" asked my father.

Mrs. Armstrong gave him a candy bar and a funny look. The three of us thanked her and went next door to the Laceys'.

Mr. Lacey greeted us: "Hi there, everybody. It's nice of you to keep an eye on the girls, Smith."

"I came along for the candy," grunted my father holding out his bag.

Mr. Lacey laughed and winked at him. "I'd go trick-or-treating myself if I had the nerve," he said. He gave each of us a lollipop, a candy bar, and three nickels for charity.

The people next to the Laceys were new in the neighborhood. My father introduced us to the lady who answered the door. "Hi, I'm Smith Krinkle. The skyscraper here is my daughter, Cindy. The surprise package is her friend, Patti."

"Nice to meet you," said the lady. "I'm Deborah Roth." She gave us two candies each. "This seems to be a fun neighborhood," she said with a smile.

"It is," grunted my father. Then he ran down the driveway, bent over with his arms dangling, like an ape. Patti and I laughed and ran after him. I waited up for Patti because it wasn't easy to run if you were wearing a cardboard box costume, plus you had short legs.

On our way to the next house, we saw two boys who were a year younger than Patti and me and lived nearby. One was dressed like a monster, the other like a robot. As we got closer, I saw yellow stuff dripping off their costumes.

They both looked ready to cry.

My father took off his ape mask and asked, "What happened?"

"Two big kids threw eggs at us," said the boy in a robot costume.

"They're hiding behind a big tree on Oak Street," said the monster, sniffling, "and throwing eggs at every kid who walks by."

My father reached into the pockets of his airplane-cleaning uniform and took out two clean cloths. He handed them to the boys so they could wipe the egg off their costumes.

"It's terrible of those boys to ruin your Halloween," he said. "Let's make sure they don't do that to anyone else."

He thought for a minute, then told us his plan ...

The two boys, my father, Patti, and I marched over to Oak Street. Across from where the big boys were hiding, we crouched behind some bushes. The moonlight was bright enough for us to see them peeking out from behind the tree. They both wore pirate outfits, with scary-looking masks. We could hear them talking and laughing, but we were silent, and they didn't seem to notice us.

My father put his mask back on and darted across the street grunting loudly. The boys screamed. When the ape-man reached them, waving his arms and grunting even louder, they screamed more. They tried to run away, but my father had them cornered.

The boys kept shrieking, and my father kept grunting and stomping his feet and chest like an angry ape. In the bushes across the street, Patti, the robot, the monster, and I roared with laughter. I laughed especially hard when one of the big boys' pirate masks fell off. It was Roger Snooterman!

After a minute or so, my father stopped grunting. He pulled off his ape mask and called us to join him.

Roger Snooterman and his friend, Andy Something-or-Other, were cowering by the tree, shaking.

"You will not be throwing any more eggs," said my father, gathering up their egg cartons. "Halloween is a joyful holiday, and you have made these children's Halloween miserable and frightening. That is why I decided to make *you* miserable and frightened for a little while."

"I'm sorry we threw the eggs, Mr. Krinkle," said Roger Snooterman. He actually did sound sorry.

"Me too," Andy Something-or-Other said.

"I'm trying to think how you can make it up to this fine young robot and monster," said my father. "I wish I had my safari hat to help me think better."

"I guess we could give them our candy?" said Andy Something-or-Other.

"What?! I don't want—"said Roger. "Oh, all right."

So Roger and Andy emptied every last candy in their trick-or-treat bags into the younger boys' bags. The robot and monster seemed to feel a whole lot better.

My father and the other kids started walking, but I stayed behind. Ever since the Young Blue Jays hike, I had wanted to talk to Roger Snooterman, and this was my chance.

Now that my father wasn't around, Roger didn't act so apologetic. "Aren't you embarrassed to have your weirdo father running around like an ape, Cindy *Toucan* Krinkle?"

"No. I'm not!" I said. "Let me tell you something, Roger Snooterman. I don't care what sourpusses like you think about my family. They may be weird, but I'd much rather have them be weird and kind, than mean, like you!"

For once, he didn't seem to know what to say.

As I ran to catch up with my trick-or-treat group, I wondered why I had ever worried about what Roger Snooterman thought of my family.

The robot was saying something to my father: "We're lucky you showed up!"

"Cindy and I are lucky, too," said Patti. "Those boys might have thrown eggs at us!"

My father just grunted. But I could tell that under his ape mask he was smiling.

We all trick-or-treated together at a bunch of houses. We saw kids in all kinds of costumes. And we each got a big haul of candy.

When our trick-or-treat bags got almost too heavy to carry, we decided to go home. My father and I walked the other kids to their houses.

"See you in school tomorrow," Patti the surprise package called from her front door. I could see the TV on in her living room, as usual.

"Thanks for making Halloween so much fun," I said to my father. I kissed him on the rubber cheek of his mask.

"Did you know an ape can pick up a skyscraper?" He lifted me up and twirled me around in a circle, three times of course.

At home, my father and I dumped our trick-or-treat bags onto the dining room table.

"Wow, you got some of my favorite candies!" said Sarah.

"Perfect timing!" said my mother. "I just finished cooking spaghetti with tomato and pumpkin sauce. We can eat candy for appetizers."

"Great idea!" I said. "And we can have the spaghetti for dessert."

We sat around the dining room table chomping on our yummy appetizers.

"Thank you for sharing your treats, Smith and Cindy," said my mother.

"Yeah, fwank oo," said Sarah with her mouth stuffed.

"If we fill up on candy," said my mother, "we can eat the spaghetti for breakfast tomorrow."

There are definitely advantages to having a weird family, I thought.

Author's Note

Since ME AND THE WEIRDOS was published back in 1981, I've received many fan letters from children across the US and other countries, even long after the book was in print. One day, I received a sweet, beautifully written email from Eva Perkins and Ashley Berrett, high school seniors in Blanding, a small town in southeastern Utah. They explained that the book had been a favorite of Eva's mom and had then become one of their favorites.

They asked my permission to turn the book into a musical. I gladly said yes, and several months later, they invited me to provide feedback on their script, ME AND THE KRINKLES.

As I read, I was blown away! The dialogue and stage directions were brilliant. The song lyrics were clever and perfectly complemented the plot. The jokes were laugh-aloud funny.

These talented young playwrights changed parts of the book to make them more stage-friendly. They softened the personality of the book's villain, Roger Snooterman, hinting that his insults aimed at the protagonist arise from his crush on her—a smart dramatic decision for their middle school cast. They portrayed this initially unlikeable character as capable of changing and growing. Yes!

As the girls and I conferred on the script across 2400 miles, my friends and family members kept saying, "You should go see the play!" *I would love to,* I thought, *but Blanding is so far away! And the performance will be in January, with who-knows-what kind of weather.*

Well, my husband and I attended the premiere, and we are so glad we did! It was delightful—entertaining, moving, and amazingly professional. Not only did Eva and Ashley write the script and song lyrics, compose the music, and conceive the staging, they cast and directed the terrific middle school actors, and even designed the posters and programs. We also received a warm welcome from Eva's and Ashley's families and the whole town of Blanding!

It's deeply touching to me that the heartfelt message of the humorous book I wrote so long ago, that it's OK—and even a *good* thing—to be different, still has an impact.

Eva's and Ashley's musical inspired me to get the book back in print. I am very grateful to Doreen Buchinski for her book design and for creating the charming cover and illustrations for this new edition. It has the same characters and plot as the original, but I've edited, tightened, and tweaked, to make it even better.

For information about obtaining the script and music for the musical **ME AND THE KRINKLES**, email meandthekrinklesmusical@gmail.com

Author of 11 books for children, **Jane Sutton** is a writing teacher, tutor and school presenter. She was elected to Phi Beta Kappa and Class Comedienne, perhaps a rare combination. Jane and her husband, Alan, live in Lexington, Massachusetts. Their grown son and daughter and their families all live in the Boston area, despite Jane's having frequently embarrassed her children when they were growing up.

Jane's website: www.jane-sutton.com

Doreen Buchinski combined pencil with digital painting to bring the illustrations for *Me and the Weirdos* to life. Doreen has a graphic design degree and also designed this book. She is the designer as well as a contributing illustrator for *An Assortment of Animals: A Children's Poetry Anthology (Fall 2018)*. In addition to illustrating, Doreen loves dogs and her garden. Doreen, her husband, and their adult children all live in Massachusetts.

Doreen's website: www.doreenbuchinski.com

94632968R00068

Made in the USA
Middletown, DE
20 October 2018